A

THE FATE OF ENDILLOE

THE TORRENT OF WATER LEAPED OUT SWIFT AND STRAIGHT
AS A SHAFT OF LIGHT.

P. 265.

Frontispiece.

THE
FATE OF ENDILLOE

BY

SILAS K. HOCKING

AUTHOR OF

"THE STRANGE ADVENTURES OF ISRAEL PENDRAY," "THE DAY OF RECOMPENSE,"
"GOD'S OUTCAST," "TO PAY THE PRICE," ETC.

WITH ORIGINAL ILLUSTRATIONS BY LANCELOT SPEED

LONDON
FREDERICK WARNE AND CO.
AND NEW YORK
1901

08472413

PRINTED BY
WILLIAM CLOWES AND SONS, LIMITED,
LONDON AND BECCLES.

CONTENTS

CONTENTS

THE FATE OF ENDILLOE

CHAPTER I

FAMILY PRIDE

> "It is not empty vanity
> To prize the name you bear."

"I HATE the whole business; and I know I shall hate the people, with their stuck-up, London ways."

"I don't know why you should, Justin," his mother answered, in hurt tones; "it seems to me you ought to be very thankful."

"I know I ought," was the impatient reply; "that is the annoying part of it. The money will be welcome enough, Heaven knows; but think of the annoyance, the inconvenience, the— the—— "

"I knew what you would say, Justin," his mother interposed, mildly; "but pride is poor fuel to boil the crock with. Besides, if any one suffers any inconvenience, it will not be you. Dorothy and I will have to bear the brunt of that."

"Of course you will," he answered, in milder tones. "But don't you see that that doesn't mend matters in the least? I would a hundred times rather slave myself than see you slaving."

"We are not going to kill ourselves, Justin. You need not fear that. Besides, it is only a matter of two months, and we shall drop back into the old ways again."

"I'm not so sure of that," he answered, slowly. "These innovations and disturbances never leave things exactly as they were before. Next year, very likely, you'll want to let the rooms again. Having made a beginning, it will be easy to go on. And then——"

"Yes, and then, Justin?" she questioned, sharply. "There's nothing dishonourable that I know of in letting part of your house during the summer, especially when seasons are bad and money is scarce. Besides, the Lovedays will not be like ordinary lodgers. I shall look upon them in the light of paying guests. You know what Cousin Phil says about them."

"I do. I wish he had said less. These London nabobs expect to be waited upon hand and foot. Paying guests, indeed! They'll regard you as a paid servant."

"You know nothing about it, Justin. You might at least wait until they arrive. It doesn't follow because they are rich that they won't know how to behave."

"I know more than you think," he answered, shortly. "When Phil was down at Easter, we had long talks together, and he told me how those London swells live. Look at Phil himself, and he wasn't to the manner born, and yet it's easy to see what he thinks of us now."

"If Phil had been to the manner born, as you call it, he would not put on so many airs and graces," was the quick reply. "That's the worst of those people who get on so fast. For a genuine snob, commend me to some one who was dug out of the gutter."

Justin laughed and shrugged his shoulders. "That's a bit hard on your own relatives, isn't it?" he questioned.

"Relatives or no, there's no denying that Phil was dragged up in a rough-and-ready fashion. That wasn't poor Mary's fault, for she died when he was a baby. We none of us thought anything of Passmore, and were all sorry when she married him."

"He managed to give Phil a good start, anyhow."

"He managed to do nothing of the sort. He died heavily in debt, as everybody knows. Phil has been fortunate, though I don't deny he's clever as well."

"Of course he's clever. Why, he's getting a thousand a year at the present time, if he's getting a penny, and here am I passing rich on a pound a week."

"My dear boy, a man may be just as happy on a pound a week as on twenty pounds a week."

"Yes; I've heard that before," was the reply. "Nevertheless, I would like to try the twenty pounds a week just by way of experiment. I confess I'm getting sick of grubbing along in this humdrum way from year to year, especially when we've to take in lodgers to help things out."

"Nobody said we were compelled to take in lodgers, Justin. Your father objected to it at first. But you know the farm is doing badly this season, and Dorothy and I thought we might as well make a few pounds when we had the chance. Three pounds a week for eight weeks running is not to be sneered at."

"I know that very well, mother; but don't you see how humiliating it is to father and to me that we are not able to earn enough between us to keep things going as we would like? Ah, if I were only earning a quarter of what Phil gets, there would be no talk of taking in lodgers."

"Your father says nothing about humiliation. He seems to have less pride than his son. He thinks if you earn what you earn honestly, nothing else is worth troubling about."

"Between pride and a reasonable self-respect," Justin said, shortly, "there is a difference. I own I dislike the idea of letting apartments, for we have carried our heads pretty high in the past. And I dislike especially letting them to people who are used to something so totally different. I can fancy how Miss Loveday will turn up her little nose with scorn at our primitive ways, and old-fashioned furniture, and country methods of doing things. I hope, at any rate, she will let off none of her criticisms in my hearing."

"You needn't see her that I know of, Justin, or any of the others. They will have the front part of the house, and we shall live in the back. The front door and the front stairs will be for their exclusive use while they are here, so you needn't worry."

"I sincerely hope I shall not see them," was the hasty reply. "I know, if I do, I shall have a difficulty in being civil."

"I think you are very unreasonable, Justin. You have taken a prejudice against people you have never seen, and are prepared to listen to nothing in their defence."

"I expect I am a bit unreasonable," he said, after a pause, rising slowly to his feet. "Any-how, I will make a point of keeping out of their way;" and he turned and walked out of the room.

In the open air he felt in a less captious frame of mind. It was a fresh, breezy evening in late June. The scent of newly-cut hay filled the atmosphere. The old orchard that stretched away from the back of the house to the foot of the slope seemed alive with twittering birds, and over all lay the soft glamour of the evening sunshine.

For awhile he loitered in the orchard, and interested himself in examining the young apples, some of which were already beginning to show a touch of red on their cheeks. Then he climbed over a stile at the far end, and began to ascend the slope towards a plantation of firs that crowned the summit, and sheltered the old farm-house from the north-westerly gales.

At the edge of the plantation he paused and turned round, and, leaning his shoulder against a rail fence, surveyed with a little thrill of pride the quiet pastoral scene that lay at his feet. Endilloe had been the home of the Pentyres for half a dozen generations at least, and because the house, together with the garden, orchard, and several meadows was freehold, they had been people of some distinction in the neighbourhood, for owners of freehold were few and far between.

There was a tradition that an earlier Pentyre

owned a hundred acres of land besides, contiguous to the house and garden, but that a great county magnate, who owned nearly the whole of the parish of St. Iago, with a number of other parishes, disputed his title, and succeeded at length in wresting the farm from him, and adding it to his own possessions.

Anyhow, the hundred acres of land that surrounded Endilloe were rented to-day, and heavily rented, too.   And it was this that kept the Pentyres on the edge of respectable poverty and sent Justin into the neighbouring town of Trelford to earn the munificent sum of fifty-two pounds ten shillings per annum as principal salesman at a seed, manure, and agricultural implement store.

Justin was a high-spirited young fellow, having a full share of pride and considerable faith in his own abilities if fortune would only give him a chance of exercising them.

At present he believed he was buried alive. There was no scope for any kind of ability at Trelford.   The little town was asleep six days out of seven.   It was only on market days that it showed any sign of being awake.   Then farmers drove in from all the country round to make their purchases and sell their farm produce.   Then their wives and daughters sat in rows in the tiny market-house, with baskets of

butter and eggs on their knees. Then boys and
maidens who had half-holiday or were " out of
work " walked into the town to enjoy themselves.
Then the shopkeepers put on their best clothes
and smiled benignly on all their customers.
Then the store—in which Justin held so con-
spicuous a place—put on its most festive look,
and every one appeared to be in the greatest
hurry, whether customers were present or
absent—for it was a tradition among the shopkeepers of Trelford that the best way of attract-
ing customers was to appear to be overwhelm-
ingly busy. Moreover, it was a tradition
founded on experience. Customers were known
to fight shy of shops where nothing appeared to
be " going on," and it was even hinted that
certain tradesmen arranged for their friends and
domestics even to stand round in their shops in
slack times so as to give an appearance of great
commercial activity.

Justin—though he loathed the weekly hypo-
crisy, and longed to get away from the narrow,
niggling life to which he was doomed—was quite
an expert in giving an appearance of activity
even in the slackest hours of that weekly market-
day. In fact, he had earned the reputation of
being the smartest salesman in Trelford; and
so much did his employers value his services
that they had, unsolicited, raised his salary

from fifty pounds a year to fifty-two pounds ten.

But though he had practically reached the top of the tree he was very far from being satisfied. True, it was better than working a rack-rented farm on insufficient capital, as his father and grandfather had done before him.

He was thankful that he had broken the succession of farmers. If the hundred acres his father farmed had been freehold, as it was originally, he would gladly have stepped into his father's shoes and handed on the succession. But to toil year in and year out for the enrichment of a man who was rich to rottenness already; to see all the value of improvements claimed by the owner, who never lifted a finger to improve his own property—that he would never consent to.

He told his father, the day after he left school, that he would go to sea, or enlist as a soldier, or work underground in the mines; but a farmer he never would be, and that nothing on earth should compel him.

He quite expected that this outburst would be met by strong coercive measures. But to his surprise his father smiled sadly, and said—

"Very well, Justin, I shall not force you into it."

"Then you are not angry with me?"

B

"No, my lad. If you can find an easier way through the world, find it by all means. There's no pleasure in farming in these days."

"Is there ever any pleasure in it?" the boy asked.

"There might be. I can conceive of nothing more delightful under some circumstances. To watch the seeds shoot, and the trees bud, and the corn ripen; to listen to the cackling of the poultry and the bleating of the lambs; to stand in the soft summer rain when the earth is dry and watch it drinking up the moisture; to lie awake of summer nights and hearken to the corncrake in the far-off fields. Ah! my boy, what can be finer than that? But when you remember that the fruit of your toil is not yours; that the lambs and the corn and the fruit have all to be sold to pay a rent that the land will not bear; that you plod, and plan, and pinch yourself from January to Christmas to find yourself at the end of the year poorer than at the beginning; that if you make an improvement or find a more remunerative market for your produce your rent is raised at the next letting day—well, under circumstances like these, there is no joy in it. The people who do nothing, and who, in the sight of Heaven, have no more right to the land than you have, reap all the fruit of your toil, and you grub your way to the grave in weariness and despair."

Justin looked up at his father in wonder. He had never heard him make so long a speech before, nor one that was so tinged with bitterness; for John Pentyre was a meek and gentle-spirited man, who was rarely heard to complain, and who accepted his lot with patient resignation.

"Then you will let me try to get my living in some other way?" the boy asked at length.

"Yes, my lad, try your best. I think I can trust you not to do anything foolish."

So, on the following day, the lad went to Trelford and engaged himself as an errand-boy, and so had worked himself up to his present position.

Justin thought of all this as he leant against the fence and looked down upon the quiet homestead nestling among the fruit trees at his feet.

Yet there was no feeling of exultation in his heart. Part of his salary also went to pay the rent, and now, as a last humiliation, lodgers were to be taken, and the best rooms in the house were to be handed over to strangers.

CHAPTER II

A WAGER

> "The life of every man is a diary
>   In which he means to write one story
>   And writes another."

A few evenings later, on his return from Trelford, his sister Dorothy met him at the garden gate.

"You had better come round to the back door, Justin," she said, in a half-whisper. "Our visitors have arrived."

"Oh, indeed——" Then he paused suddenly. Other words were on the tip of his tongue, but second thoughts came to his rescue. Nothing was to be gained by making himself disagreeable, especially as upon Dorothy and his mother would fall the bulk of the worry and inconvenience.

"I know you don't like it," Dorothy went on. "You think it is humiliating; but I don't see why. Everybody does it nowadays. You see, Cornwall is becoming quite popular, and I don't

18

see why we should not take advantage of the vogue and make hay while the sun shines."

"I don't like to see you turned into a waitress, Dorothy," he said, with a smile; "but if you don't mind, it is not for me to complain."

"Oh, I don't mind in the least," she said, brightly; "indeed, I think I shall enjoy it for a change. But, do you know, I was terribly nervous before they came."

"And now?" he questioned.

"Why, you will scarcely believe it, but I feel as though I had known them a long time already."

"I suppose they have patronized you and called you by your Christian name? Just like those purse-proud nobodies with their familiar ways."

"Now you are making yourself nasty, Justin, and assuming what isn't true. Nobody could have been nicer, and they have treated me with every respect. Why will you be so prejudiced against people that you know nothing about?"

"I don't know, Dorothy; it is very foolish of me, no doubt. But is supper ready? for I am terribly hungry in spite of the heat."

"It's ready and waiting. But don't be long over it, for I want you to take me for a walk. I've been in the house the whole of the day; and, besides, I have a lot to tell you."

"All right. You remain in the orchard till I come out;" and he disappeared suddenly into the house.

Dorothy walked up and down under the trees swinging her straw hat in her hand. The sun was setting behind the plantation, and decorating the uppermost boughs with long streaks of vermilion and gold. Nearly all the fields lay in shadow, and in the orchard a cool wind stirred and awoke low whispers among the leaves. It was an ideal summer evening—cool and fragrant after the sultry heat of a cloudless day.

Justin took full time over his supper, but Dorothy showed no impatience. It was just delightful to loiter under the trees and listen to the sparrows chirping in all directions and feel the soft breath of the wind stirring the straying locks of soft brown hair that lay so lightly upon her brow. Delightful, too, to dream her maiden dreams and weave all manner of pleasant fancies, and see her castles rising in the air great, and noble, and strong.

She was of a hopeful temperament, for in reality there was not much prospect of any of her dreams being realized. But it was not her nature to argue out such questions. She was young, and a woman ; and it is of the very genius of youth to fling rainbow arches across impassable ravines, and of the indestructible nature of a woman to hope when all ground of hope has been taken away.

Dorothy had her silent hours of sorrow, when her lips trembled in spite of herself, and the tears were abundant upon her cheeks; but she never despaired. Her hope was as constant as the daylight, and what to others were proven facts were to her but idle dreams, which the unfolding of some future day would scatter to the winds.

Justin came out at length, and without a word they walked away together. Dorothy took his arm as they climbed the slope. But they did not speak until they got into the heart of the plantation. By this time the sun had disappeared, but the sky was still aflame with his light, and the wind was humming merrily in the tree tops.

A few minutes' brisk walking and they came out on the other side of the plantation, and in a moment the whole scene was changed. Right and left stretched a heathery common, destitute of tree or shrub, and in front lay the great ocean still and almost silent, like a monster fast asleep.

"The sea scarcely moans to-night," Dorothy said, as she stood on the brink of the cliff and looked down. "Hearken, Justin, did you hear that deep note? or, rather, did you feel it, for it is almost too deep to be heard?"

"Old Neptune is dreaming," he said, with a smile. "Look out yonder by the headland and see how his bosom heaves. After all the mischief he has wrought, it is no wonder that he sleeps uneasily."

"And yet we love the great restless creature," Dorothy answered, with her eyes still fixed on the rising tide below. Then she turned suddenly. "It's too much trouble to go down on the rocks," she said. "Let's sit here on the heather."

"It would be too much trouble to climb up again," he answered, following her. "Besides, I thought you had a lot to tell me?"

"So I have when we can find a comfortable seat. Ah, here is an armchair, cushioned and complete;" and she sat down suddenly in a bank of heather.

In a few moments he was seated by her side, and they were looking off upon the trackless ocean, that was growing solemn and mysterious under the gathering shadows.

"Did it ever occur to you, Dorothy," he said, "that modern discovery has robbed the world of nearly all its romance?"

"No," she answered, demurely. "And I don't think I know exactly what you mean."

"I mean that, as far as the world itself is concerned, there is little or nothing more to find out. Think of how this great ocean would appeal to our forefathers! It was a mystery unmeasured and unexplored to them. They would stand here on these very cliffs and wonder what lay out there beyond the sunset—wonder if there were other lands or other worlds, or if the sea stretched away for ever. What scope there was for the romancers of those days, what a field for the imagination! But there's no room for romance any more. Those shadows out there on the horizon don't impress me with any sense of mystery. I know the size of the ocean and the shape of it. I do not wonder what lies beyond. I know America is out there on the slope of the circle. We've measured up all the oceans, and explored all the continents, and made a chart of the bottom of the sea, and there's nothing left to wonder about or excite the imagination."

"Oh, that's all nonsense, Justin," she said, in her quiet way. "You have not seen the world when you've looked at a map, nor all that is in it because you have been to Wombwell's wild-beast show. I really think it is time you had a change of air."

"I think so myself," he answered, with a laugh; "but, unfortunately, there's no such luck. A pound a week won't run to such luxuries."

"No, I suppose not. But let us not get on

to that subject, please. I want to talk to you about something much more pleasant."

"That's good of you. I'm all attention."

"Do you remember saying last week that you would wager your Sunday hat Miss Loveday was a vinegary female of uncertain age, and dowered with a long catalogue of ailments?"

"Did I say so much?"

"You did. As a matter of fact, you said a great deal more, but I've forgotten the rest; not that that matters, for it was not worth remembering."

"No? Then you've done wisely, my sweet sister, in forgetting."

"I know that very well. But what I want to impress upon you is, the foolishness of prophesying until you know."

"May I ask if that remark is original?" he inquired, with mock seriousness.

"No, you may not. You want to turn me off on a side issue again, but I'm not going to let you. I expect you to bring me a new hat from Trelford to-morrow, and don't let it be a shabby one, either."

"Oh, my!" he said, with a laugh, "this is getting serious. But let me see where we are. You say that I wagered my Sunday hat that Miss Loveday was an elderly spinster."

"Exactly, and you've lost."

"But, as far as I remember, you did not accept the wager."

"And if I didn't, that's nothing to do with it. You said what wasn't true, and so you've lost."

"In that case, then, I shall have to give you my Sunday hat."

"Your Sunday hat, indeed;" and she laughed a low, silvery laugh. "But you are just like a man, Justin, you seem unable to see a plain issue when it is placed before you."

"I'm afraid that is true," he answered, trying to look grave. "But, admitting your distinctly feminine argument to be conclusive up to the present point, I fail to see, even now, how you have established your claim."

"Well, I never. How blind you must be!"

"Granted that that is true," he answered, in the same bantering tone, "still, you have given me no proof that what I said was not correct."

"No proof? Haven't I told you that she is the very opposite?"

"Your testimony is valuable, no doubt, my dear sister; still, it is not proof."

"Oh, isn't it?" was the ready answer. "Do you think I've no eyes, or that I don't know how to use them? I tell you, Ruby Loveday is the prettiest creature you ever saw, and she isn't more than nineteen if she's a day."

"And is this the news you were so eager to communicate?" he questioned.

"I wanted to prove to you how stupid and prejudiced you have been. From the very first you made up your mind that the Lovedays would be disagreeable people. Well, they are nothing of the sort, they are the very opposite, in fact; and as for Ruby—well, all I can say is you had better remain out of her way if you wish to keep heart-whole."

"I intend to keep out of their way," he answered, "but not for any such reason as you suggest. To begin with, I don't want to be patronized or asked to run errands, and in the next place, I have no interest in people whom I have never seen, and who, when they leave here, we shall never see again."

Dorothy rose to her feet and laughed. "Look here, Justin," she said, "I'll wager that new hat you owe me that before a month is over you'll be more interested in the Lovedays than any of us."

"Indeed. But I thought you advised me just now not to prophesy?"

"So I did. And I tell you again you should never do so, for you are always miles and miles out when you try."

"Don't you think you would be safe in following your own advice?"

"Not in this case, for I know what I am talking about. What I am afraid of is that you will fall head over heels in love, and then the last state of that man will be worse than the first."

"It would be very much worse," he answered, with a smile. "But you needn't fear, Dorothy. If I ever fall in love it will not be with a city miss. I shall need a wife, if ever I marry, who understands housekeeping, and who knows the value of a shilling."

"Well, then, you had better keep out of Ruby Loveday's way, for she has the sweetest and the most bewitching eyes you ever saw. I tell you I'm half in love with her myself; and you know girls don't think much of girls as a rule. But Ruby Loveday is just lovely; she is indeed. She is as dainty as a spring flower, and as graceful as a fawn; not that I know what a fawn is, but it's the proper kind of simile I know."

"Yes, go on," he said, with another laugh; "the simile is quite appropriate. What other good qualities does she possess?"

"Oh, she's sweet tempered, I'm sure she is, and good, and kind. I'm sure you'll fall in love with her, Justin."

"I hope not, Dorothy. And as the chances are I shall not see her there does not seem to be much danger in that direction."

"Well, your only hope is to keep out of the

way.   But who comes here, I wonder?" and she stepped aside and peered into the shadowy plantation.   "It's the Lovedays, as I'm alive!" she whispered.   "They've come out to explore the neighbourhood and catch a glimpse of the sea before it grows quite dark.   There's no escape for you, Justin, so steel your heart and do the agreeable at the same time."

CHAPTER III

RUBY

"She's all my fancy painted her ;
She's lovely, she's divine."

JUSTIN had no occasion to steel his heart, however, for Ruby was not of the party. She was
too tired for a walk, after her long railway
journey, and preferred to remain in the house
and finish a book she was reading.

Mr. Loveday caught sight of Dorothy directly
he emerged from the plantation, and came at
once towards her, followed by Mrs. Loveday
and Nathan Hendy, Mr. Pentyre's hind and man-
of-all-work.

Nathan was only too pleased to assume the
position of guide, philosopher, and friend to the
new arrivals from London, and to show them all
the beauties of Endilloe and surrounding neighbourhood. Nathan was something of an oracle
in his way, and, like most such oracles, believed
that people who were born and brought up in

cities were in a state of the most lamentable and pitiable ignorance. This thesis Nathan had proved again and again—to his own satisfaction, at any rate, if not to the satisfaction of other people, and was prepared to prove it again on the shortest possible notice.

"Take pigs," Nathan would say, "by way of example. Now, what do townspeople know 'bout pigs ? As a fact, they don't knaw nothin'. Why, a chap from some big town up the country wance axed me ef we sheared 'em for wool. Then take the weather. Their hignorance on that subject es terrible—an' the wust is they keep puttin' of it in the papers. But there ! what can ee expect from people brought up in sich places ?"

In this way Nathan would defend his pro-position against all comers, and in his heart thanked Heaven that he had been born in the country and not in any of those benighted towns. The advent of his master's paying guests Nathan hailed with great pleasure, and was delighted that on the very first evening he had the opportunity of showing them round the neighbourhood.

It was a little disappointment to Nathan that they asked to be taken straight to the sea. He had so many other things to show them of far greater interest. There were pigs, and poultry, and sheep, and a prize heifer, to say nothing of various crops in the fields.

But, no. The tall, handsome gentleman, in his light check suit and cloth cap, had no wish to be taken into the yard or the fields. He wanted to get on the cliffs at the nearest point, where he could smell the salt air and enjoy the sight of the sea, and his wife was as eager for the sea as himself.

"Jist like those townsfolk," was Nathan's unspoken comment. "They're jist like ducks— they make for the watter fust thing; but then, what can 'ee expect of people brought up in sich places?"

So Nathan, in a very demure, not to say sorrowful, frame of mind, led the way up the slope and through the plantation, until they came out upon the cliffs. Then, to make matters worse, Mr. Loveday appeared to forget his presence. Dorothy at once claimed his attention, then Justin was introduced, and in a few minutes the four of them were standing in a row looking off upon the darkening stretch of ocean, and talking as freely as though they had known each other all their lives.

Nathan stood solitary and alone, fifty yards away. Then reflecting that he was not wanted, turned slowly and retraced his steps to Endilloe.

Justin, notwithstanding all his protestations

C

to Dorothy, was considerably disappointed that the young lady had not come out with her parents. Whether Dorothy had intended it or no, she had succeeded in rousing his curiosity. A pretty maiden is always an interesting object to a young man, and after all that Dorothy had said, he would have been less than human had he not felt more or less curious to see such a dainty and bewitching creature.

He soon forgot his disappointment, however. Mr. and Mrs. Loveday proved to be such agreeable company that he was sorry when the slowly gathering darkness compelled them to return. It is true they talked about nothing in particular. But the charm of conversation is not so much in the matter as in the manner. Mr. Evan Loveday was a capable, well-read, up-to-date city man, and he pretended to be nothing more nor less. That he had been successful—after the manner of what the world calls success—there could be no doubt; but purse-proud he was not.

Justin found all his prognostications falsified during the first five minutes. The city merchant and the country salesman met on equal ground. The question of social difference did not occur to either of them, least of all to Evan Loveday; and when they parted at the orchard gate, Justin found all his prejudices scattered to the winds.

"Well," questioned Dorothy, when the Love-days were out of hearing, "what is your verdict?"

"I must confess they are very agreeable people," he answered.

"I thought you would say so. But what a providence for you that Ruby did not come out."

"Why so?"

"Because you would have lost your heart by this time;" and she ran laughing into the house.

In the big roomy kitchen which had now to answer the double purpose of dining-room and drawing-room, Mrs. Pentyre and her husband were discussing with great animation the advent of the strangers, or more particularly the advent of Ruby. For as yet John Pentyre had not seen Mr. and Mrs. Loveday.

Ruby, it would appear, having finished her book, and getting tired of being alone, had come off into the kitchen in search of company. Mrs. Pentyre nearly dropped, as she expressed it, when the door silently opened, and the dainty apparition, most bewitchingly attired, advanced into the room. John rose from his seat in the big chimney-nook, and took his pipe slowly from between his teeth, much wondering what was the proper thing for him to do or say under the circumstances. Not being able to answer that question satisfactorily, he stood stock-still, and said nothing.

"Why, my dear," said Mrs. Pentyre, in her motherly way, lifting up her hands deprecatingly, "a kitchen with a stone floor is not the proper place for such as you!"

"Oh, I don't mind the stone floor in the least!" was the smiling answer; "but what a dear, glorious old room! You won't mind my coming in, will you?"

"Oh dear, no; come, and welcome. John, get a chair for the young lady."

"No; please, Mr. Pentyre, don't trouble. I'm quite rested now. Father and mother, you know, have gone off in search of the sea."

"Yes, I know. I sent Nathan to show them the way."

"Is it far?" she questioned, looking up at him with a smile.

"Oh no; just over the top of the hill beyond the plantation. But the easiest way to get on the beach is to go down the valley, which twists round into Poldula Porth."

"I felt too tired to go myself," she answered, after a pause; "besides, I wanted to finish my book, and then I shall have plenty of time to see everything, shan't I?"

"Oh yes, I hope so," he answered, slowly, still holding his pipe between his finger and thumb, and wondering if it would be considered rude to finish it in her presence. She was only a girl—and a mere slip of a girl at that, as he admitted to himself afterwards. Yet somehow he felt considerably overawed in her presence. "Oh yes, you will have plenty of time," he went on, uneasily; "for, after all, there isn't much to be seen in a place like this. I'm afraid you'll find it terrible dull."

"Oh, I don't think so at all—not if the weather keeps fine! But won't you finish your pipe? I'm sure you are letting it go out."

"Then you won't mind my smoking?" he said, brightly, and smiling at her.

"Oh dear, no! Father smokes like a Thames ferry-boat, and that's saying a great deal, isn't it?"

"Well, very likely it is, miss," he said, doubtfully; "very likely it is; but having never seen a Thames ferry-boat——"

"Now, John, you needn't show off your ignorance before the young lady," Mrs. Pentyre interrupted, somewhat reproachfully. "But it's this way, miss," she continued, turning towards Ruby, "I've been trying for years to get him to take me to London, but he keeps putting it off. I expect some day I shall go without him."

"You'd soon want to get back again, I fancy," Ruby said, with a smile. "London is a frightfully dull place. We once spent a whole summer in London. Father could not get away, for some reason. Well, believe me, it was worse than the heart of Africa.   Everybody goes away in August, you see—— But your pipe is out, Mr. Pentyre; allow me. I nearly always light father's cigars when I have the chance. There now——"

Mrs. Pentyre held up her hands in consternation. To think a young lady from London should strike a match and hold it over the bowl of her husband's pipe until it was alight, while he quietly submitted as though he enjoyed being waited upon! It was outrageous! She felt too astonished to speak.

"My! But you have pretty little hands, miss!" he said, eyeing her taper fingers admiringly. "I reckon you never did very much hard work." Then he caught his wife's eye and blushed uncomfortably.

"John!" That was all she said; but there was no mistaking the tone, and it spoke volumes to him.

For several minutes after that John smoked in silence, while Ruby explored the great kitchen, under the guidance of Mrs. Pentyre, and ultimately disappeared into the dairy to have a look at the butter and cream.

When the door closed behind them, and he found himself alone in the great kitchen, he fell to thinking. The sight of this fresh, girlish face stirred his heart with old memories. He found

himself back again in the days of his youth,
living over again those sweet hours of romance
that remain among the most priceless of the
memories of life.

When Ruby returned, his pipe was out again,
for he could not smoke and dream at the same
time.

It was in vain that he protested, in vain that
Mrs. Pentyre tried to catch his eye. Ruby persisted in re-lighting the pipe, and John admired
the white taper fingers a second time, but was
careful not to make any remark. But in his
heart he said, "Bless her; she's a little beauty."

When Dorothy and Justin returned, Mrs.
Pentyre had got beyond the rebuke stage, and
John felt himself at liberty to enlarge on the
many charms of their fair visitor.

"You ought to have been here, Justin," he
said to his son, pulling deep whiffs at his
pipe; "she's a sight for weak eyes; she is
indeed!"

"So she's captured you also, has she?" he
said, indifferently. "I really think I'd better
keep out of the way."

"That's just what I have been telling you,"
Dorothy interposed, banteringly. "If you take
my advice, you will stick to your first resolution."

"As far as I know, there is no reason why
I should not," he answered, "though I am not

afraid of any ill effects following my meeting her."

"But, joking apart," interposed Mrs. Pentyre, "she is really one of the sweetest little creatures I've ever seen, and hasn't one bit of pride——"

"Not a bit," interposed John, with emphasis.

"And as free and friendly as if we were her equals——"

"You'd hardly think it, but she would insist on lighting my pipe," interrupted John.

"And her dress—well, you should have seen it, Dorothy. Of course, it was not fit for a kitchen——"

"But her hands caught my fancy," John remarked from out the chimney nook.

"Yes. And, do you know, he told her so," said Mrs. Pentyre, severely, after which conversation became more general.

Soon after, Justin went off to bed, for he had to be early astir in the morning. But, try as he would, he could not keep the name of Ruby out of his mind. He had pretended to Dorothy that he did not want to see their fair visitor, and that it was his deliberate intention to keep out of her way. Yet all the time, in spite of himself, he kept drawing imaginary pictures of her, and endowing her with more virtues than even her most intimate friends ever discovered in her.

He acknowledged to himself that this was

exceedingly silly, and quite unworthy of a man who, up to the age of twenty-two, had kept himself heart-whole and fancy free. But, silly or not, there was no denying the fact that this unseen and unknown stranger had already begun to exercise an uncomfortable influence upon his mind.

Of course, it was all Dorothy's fault. If Dorothy had said nothing about her, and his father and mother had also remained silent, he would scarcely have given to her a first thought, much less a second. It was humiliating to be kept awake on the very first night by one whom he had never seen.

CHAPTER IV

DISAPPOINTMENT

> " My curiosity gets the better of me,
> And steals my sleep."

DURING the next week it seemed to Justin as though Miss Loveday deliberately kept out of his way. Try as he would, he could not get a glimpse of her. When he left in the morning she was not yet stirring, and when he returned in the evening she was either engrossed with a book or else had gone off on some excursion with her father and did not return until after dark, so that by the end of a week he had not so much as seen the flutter of one of her pretty frocks.

This was all the more annoying since the other members of the family saw her constantly, and had something to say every evening relative to her sweetness and good nature. Justin listened to her praises in dogged silence, and pretended not to be in the least interested ; though he was, in reality, much more piqued than he would have admitted even to himself.

He began to think after awhile that Miss Ruby had either overheard his conversation with Dorothy or else that Dorothy had inadvertently or unconsciously betrayed his sentiments, and that the stranger was, in consequence, standing on her dignity and giving him to understand that she was sublimely indifferent to his existence, and was less anxious to see him than he was to see her.

He would have asked Dorothy, if he dared, if Miss Loveday was aware of his existence. But he could not do that without betraying an interest that he had all along professed he did not feel. If he had talked less beforehand, he need not have been so reticent now. He was being well paid out for his pride and stupidity.

He made one or two earnest attempts to banish the subject from his mind. After all, what did it matter to him? The Lovedays did not belong to his world. From what his cousin, Phil Pasmore, had said, they were rich people, and lived in considerable style somewhere in the West End of London. They had come to Endilloe for a couple of months for change of air and rest —though it was understood that Mr. Loveday would go up to town every now and then on business—and when the time was up they would go back to London again, and in all probability they would never see them or hear of them again. Under the circumstances, what did it matter to him if he never saw Miss Loveday? And it was worse than foolishness to waste a single thought upon her.

But though his reasoning was eminently sound, and no one could cast doubt on the wisdom of his resolutions, he was not long in discovering, what most people have discovered, that human nature is not to be ruled by logic, and that if reason says you should not go a certain way that is the way of all others you most desire to go.

Justin looked at all the front windows every morning, when leaving for Trelford, particularly at the window of the room that Miss Loveday occupied, but the blind was invariably down. Evidently she was not particularly fond of early rising. Thursday was early-closing day at Trelford, and as he hurried homeward between two and three in the afternoon he felt quite confident that that day, at any rate, his curiosity would be rewarded. Dorothy came to meet him, as her custom was when she was not busy.

"You ought to have got home an hour earlier, Justin," she said, "and then you would have seen the Lovedays drive off in style."

"Gone, have they?" he questioned, with a curious sensation of sinking at the heart.

"They've driven over to Newquay, to visit some friends of theirs who are staying there."

"Where did they get a carriage?"

"Had it sent over from Trelford; and a handsome turn-out it was—coachman in livery and a splendid pair of horses. I did not think the White Hart could have done it in such good style."

"Evidently you don't know what Trelford is capable of," he said, with a smile.

"But the carriage was nothing to Miss Loveday. You should have seen her, Justin."

"Indeed!"

"She was a perfect picture. Really, Justin, she is the loveliest creature you ever saw."

"But I have not seen her," he said, with pretended indifference.

"That is the reason you ought to have been at home an hour earlier. She was dressed all in white — white lace dress, white boots, white ostrich feathers in her broad-brimmed leghorn hat, white gloves. You really cannot imagine how pretty she looked."

"You are quite sure she is not an angel dropped down here by mistake?"

"Don't be cynical, Justin. She's just a merry-hearted girl, as human as she can be."

"That's a contradiction, isn't it? I thought human nature was mean, and selfish, and cross."

"Oh no, Justin, not at all. You are thinking of the 'leavings' that were dealt out to you;" and she looked up into his face and laughed.

"I do think I got more than my fair share of original sin," he answered. "But what shall we do with ourselves this afternoon?"

"Oh, anything, so long as it does not require effort," she said, brightly. "It is too hot for violent exercise. Father says if the weather keeps like this harvest will be upon us directly."

People who live in the country have to be content with small things in the way of entertainments. Consequently they get into the way of entertaining themselves, and find pleasure in ways that never occur to dwellers in cities. To the *blasé* city youth there may not seem much pleasure to be extracted from a tea-drink, or a country fair, or a village feast, or a ploughing-match, or a picnic on some grassy cliff by the sea. But country-people know better; and it is to be questioned if rich and fashionable folk who pay to be entertained get as much pleasure out of theatre and card-party and dance as country-people do out of the simple pleasures they manufacture for themselves.

Justin and Dorothy spent most of the afternoon in the shadow of the orchard and plantation, and time did not hang heavy upon their hands. When the sun began to dip behind the firs that crowned the hill they went out to the cliff and sat down. It was fine to see the sun like a great ball of fire sinking into the ocean. Fine to see the clouds take fire and burn blood-red down to the very edge of the sea; fine to watch the shining track of light across the moving waters like a highway to the Celestial City.

It was late when the Lovedays got back, and Justin had gone to bed, but he fancied he heard a sweet, girlish voice singing an old love-song just as he was dropping off to sleep. Perhaps he was mistaken; he was too sleepy to inquire.

The next morning as he journeyed to Trelford he reflected that he would have to wait now until Sunday before his curiosity could be satisfied with a sight of Ruby Loveday's face. Friday was market-day, and he always got home late that evening, and Saturday was no better in that respect. It had got to be the custom of people—though they liked short hours themselves—to keep shop assistants on their feet till nearly midnight.

"But I shall see her on Sunday, at any rate," he reflected. "I wonder if they will go with us to chapel? Not very likely, I fancy. I saw it stated in some paper the other day that the West End of London knows nothing of dissent.

So most likely they will walk to St. Iago Churchtown, in which case they will start earlier than we shall, and, of course, we shall see them go."

So the long and toilsome hours of Friday and Saturday wore away, and Sunday morning dawned at length, bright and cloudless. Justin donned his Sunday best, and giving his moustache an extra twist, sauntered out into the orchard. Now and then he glanced surreptitiously over the thorn hedge at the front garden, and every time he did so he expected to see the vision of a dainty figure, clad in white, and of an exceedingly pretty face.

But disappointment still dogged his steps. Mr. and Mrs. Loveday came out into the garden, and wandered up and down for several minutes in animated conversation, but Ruby did not appear on the scene. He learnt later that she had got cold, and had been persuaded by her mother to stay in bed.

"That comes of getting her feet wet," Dorothy said, sententiously. "I told her what would happen."

"When did you tell her?" Justin questioned, with pretended indifference.

"On Friday afternoon. We scrambled down the cliff together, and hunted for crabs in the pools. You should have seen her. She was just wild with excitement, and didn't take the least notice where she was going. If the pools had been deep enough, she would have drowned herself, I verily believe."

John Pentyre laughed. "She's just as frisky as a young kitten," he said, "and a sight prettier."

Ruby came downstairs to tea, but she did not venture out of doors. Justin was ready to bite his finger-nails with disappointment. He loitered in the orchard and in the lane outside the front garden; he glanced at the window of her bedroom again and again; he even made an excuse for going into the hall, which was now used exclusively by the Lovedays, but nothing came of it all. The one face that he was aching with curiosity to see kept persistently out of sight.

Mr. and Mrs. Loveday, as he expected, went to church in the morning, and in the evening they expressed a wish to go to chapel with the Pentyres.

Justin had declared during the afternoon that he would not go to chapel a second time. Now he regretted it. He had missed a splendid opportunity of getting better acquainted with their guests, and perhaps of being invited to their rooms.

"Just my luck!" he muttered to himself; but there was no going back on it now.

D

Dorothy promised to stay at home to keep Miss Ruby company, and when Justin heard that announcement he brightened up again.

"The girls will know, of course, that I shall be in the house alone," he reflected; "so very likely they will ask me to keep them company. And if they do—why, I shall not say no."

After the elders of the two families had taken themselves off to chapel, Dorothy disappeared to keep Ruby company. Justin stationed himself near the door that opened into the passage leading to the best rooms, and waited somewhat impatiently for his sister's re-appearance.

Now and then he heard a faint hum of voices, the low ripple of laughter, and he laid his book upon his knee, and bent his ear towards the chink of the door. It was a most undignified thing to do, but he was almost consumed with curiosity.

Later he heard a step, and he pushed his chair a little distance away, and took up his book again. Dorothy came bounding into the room a minute later.

"You here still?" she questioned. "I thought you were going for a walk."

"I feel too lazy," he answered. "Besides, I did not know you were going to spend the whole evening with—that is, in the other part of the house."

"Do you want me for anything in particular?" she questioned.

"Oh no," he answered, indifferently; "and it is evident you don't want me."

"Well, not now," she said, with a smile. "The fact is, Miss Loveday and I are having a splendid time."

"So it would appear," he replied; and then Dorothy disappeared again, leaving the door ajar.

He tried his best to conquer his chagrin, and to become interested in his book; but it was a vain endeavour, especially as every now and then low ripples of laughter and snatches of conversation floated out to him.

Then the piano was opened, and a few firm chords were struck.

"Dorothy is going to sing," he said to himself.

The next moment the clear notes of a rich contralto voice seemed to fill all the house.

"I hear thee speak of a better land."

The words were as distinct as if he sat by the side of the singer.

Justin sat like one spell-bound until the song was ended, then he drew a long breath, and rose slowly to his feet. What kind of throat could a voice like that come from? he wondered. What was the singer like?

"It is evident I am not wanted," he said to himself at length, and he put on his hat and went out into the orchard.

The next morning Mr. Loveday went off to London for two or three days, and Justin took up the burden of life at the stores.

It was nearly dark when he returned on Tuesday evening, and he found the household in a state of consternation. Miss Loveday had gone out alone early in the afternoon, and had not returned. Search had been made in all directions, but no tidings of her could be gleaned. The last seen of her, she was talking with Amos Blue in the turnip field, and was then in the best of spirits; which way she went after that no one knew, for no one had seen her since. Her absence was not noticed until tea-time; but not turning up at the usual hour her mother got anxious, and that anxiety had deepened with every moment since.

CHAPTER V

A DARK ABYSS

> " I would risk a thousand lives
> And count it joy."

JUSTIN listened to all that was said without speaking a word. For the moment he felt stunned. That Mrs. Loveday had abundant reason for anxiety there could be no doubt. Miss Loveday was not likely to stay away so long unless some accident had befallen her. Still, it might not be serious, and tidings of her might come to hand at any moment.

It was not till Mrs. Loveday proposed telegraphing to her husband to return at once that Justin spoke.

"I would not, if I were you," he said. "It would make him terribly anxious, and there is no train by which he could travel to-night."

"But—but—suppose Ruby has met her—her death. Oh, he would never forgive me for keeping him in ignorance."

"But let us not suppose any such thing," Justin said quietly. "There may be a dozen explanations of her absence short of that."

"Oh, I don't know. I can't help fearing the worst. Ruby knows how anxious I always am; and, if she were alive, she would have come home or sent me word."

"She may be alive, and not able to do either," was the reply.

"You mean that she may have been kidnapped?"

"No; I don't mean that. Such a possibility has not crossed my mind. Who could kidnap her in a place like this, and for what purpose?"

"Oh, there are always gipsies loitering about; and one is constantly reading in the papers such horrible things, that—that—oh, I don't know what to think."

"Try to think that at worst your daughter has only met with a slight accident," he said slowly. "But I must join in the search. I hope we shall bring you good tidings soon."

In the yard he met Nathan, who had returned from a walk along the cliffs. Nathan looked annoyed rather than anxious.

"No, sur; there ain't no sign of her out 'long there," he said, in reply to Justin's question. "An' nobody ain't seed her out that way neither;

but, lor! what can 'ee expect of people brought up in sich a way?"

"Why, what's the bringing-up to do with it, Nathan?"

"To do with it? Why, everything to do with it, I says. You never heerd of a St. Iago woman go and lost herself in that way."

"Well?"

"No, 'tain't well toal, from my point of view. If you get thews townspeople down here, with their hup-the-country ways, there's sure to be trouble of some kind. They be that hignorant that they go into trouble straight, without knawin' it."

Justin smiled, though he felt in anything but a merry humour. It was Nathan's unshaken belief that city people were a set of igno-ramuses when compared with people whose good fortune it was to be born and bred in the country.

"Well, Nathan," he said, after a moment's pause, "we have no time to waste in argument now. Every moment may be of the utmost value. The question is, what places have been searched, and what more can be done before it gets dark?"

"Blest if I know, sur. We seem to have been everywhere likely an' unlikely. We've axed everybody we've seen if they've seen the maid;

an' as far as I can see, we'll 'ave to wait till she turns up herself."

"No, no;" Justin said, "we must not give up the search while there is any place, likely or unlikely, left unexplored."

"Well then, what be we to do furder?" Nathan asked, doggedly.

"Well, there are three places that might, under certain circumstances, be considered dangerous.   There is the river——"

"Well, she ain't tumbled in there, in my judgment.   I searched all 'long there fust thing."

"Then there are the cliffs——"

"She dedn' go that way; oal the same, I've been out there now, an' as I towld 'ee, there ain't a sign of her."

"Then there are one or two disused mine-shafts——"

"Ah, I never thought of them," Nathan said, eagerly.   "Iss, sur, we must look in they places. She might have tried to reach a ripe blackberry, or something, and overbalanced herself."

Justin shuddered.   If she had fallen into one of the shafts, he knew there was very little hope of her being got out alive.

The next moment John Pentyre came upon the scene, accompanied by three or four neigh-bouring farmers and a dozen farm-labourers.

They had been scouring the lanes and fields and ditches for the last hour, but had not come across a single sign of the missing girl.

"What about the shafts?" Justin said, with a little thrill of anxiety in his voice.

But a dead silence followed the question.

"Don't you think they ought to be searched?" he asked, after a painful pause.

"Yes, yes; we must search everywhere," John Pentyre answered at length; "but if the little maid has tumbled down a shaft, it's all up with her;" and his voice ended in a choke.

In a few moments the little company broke up into three distinct groups, and struck off across the fields in different directions. The sun had already disappeared behind the fir-crowned hill, and the purple twilight was beginning to creep up the valley. Three big mounds of rubbish, covered in the main, by brambles and furze, indicated where the treacherous shafts lay hidden.

Justin led his little party to the mound that was on the way to the sea.

"She may have decided to go out on the cliffs," he reflected, "though when she left the house she went in the opposite direction. If that be so, she would most likely take the path across the Downs, and so would pass close to the shaft, and, attracted by the profusion of

brambles and the prospect of some ripe blackberries, and not knowing there was a funnel-
shaped pit in the centre, she may have fallen
in unawares."

Justin reached the mound before any of the
others, and made a quick circuit round it; then
selecting a spot that the brambles had not
covered, he ran lightly up the bank of rubble,
and for a moment or two gazed with a kind of
fascination at the black, gaping pit not three
yards from where he stood.

The next moment a low cry escaped his lips;
almost close to his feet was a small white glove.
He stooped and picked it up, and held it out
in his hand for his companions to see.

There was a simultaneous gasp, followed by
a dumb, painful silence.

Justin was the first to speak. "I fear we
have reached the end of our search," he said,
making a desperate effort to keep his voice
steady. "She is lying at the bottom of the
shaft, you may depend."

"Poor little maid!" broke from the lips of
one of the men; and then silence fell again.

An examination of the spot revealed the fact
that the brambles had been slightly trampled
down near the spot where the glove was found,
an early blackberry evidently being the object
of the quest.

The next thing to do was to get as near the edge of the shaft as possible, and call down into its black depths, though no one expected any response, and, indeed, no response came back.

Justin called again and again, "Is any one there?" but the only reply was the dull echo of his own voice.

One of the men was for raising a shout to attract the other searchers.

"No, no," said Justin; "if you shout, the women will hear. We must go about the work as silently as possible."

"But what must us do?" questioned one of the men.

"Go and inform the others and then get ropes and ladders. The ladders we must throw across the shaft——"

"But who will slidder down a rope?" interrupted two or three at once.

"That shall be my task," said Justin, calmly. "So I will wait here till you come back, for I shall need all my strength."

When his companions had gone, Justin sat down on the bank, with his face towards Endilloe. Across the landscape the twilight was deepening rapidly, the distant hills being already lost in a purple haze. The silence was unbroken save for the harsh and dissonant voice of a corncrake that every now and then jarred upon the serene quiet of the evening.   In the village of St. Iago Church-town, that straggled up the side of the opposite hill, the lights were peeping out one by one. The cottagers were getting their evening meal. Very soon the lights would go out again, and the village would sleep in the darkness.

Behind him was the black, gaping pit, and lying at its bottom—what ?

He shuddered a little, perhaps he felt the chill of the summer evening.   The men seemed very slow in fetching the ladders and ropes. Not that it could matter very much, for if Ruby Loveday was lying at the bottom of the shaft she would be unconscious of the flight of time and untroubled by the trouble and anxiety of others.

He began to wonder after awhile if the interest he felt in the case was the interest of an ordinary stranger.   He did not remember ever being so troubled before about anything.   There had been accidents often in the parish of St. Iago.   Miners had been killed underground, and sailors had been drowned off the coast, but he had never felt in the same way about these calamities as he was feeling now.

Why was it ?   He had never spoken to Ruby Loveday, had not even seen her.   Hence she was nothing to him, not so much as the miners of St. Iago, whom he at least knew by sight. Yet somehow, his heart felt like lead, and the tears came perilously near his eyes.

It did not occur to him that, for the best part of a week, he had been half-worshipping a creation of his own imagination. The real Ruby he had never seen, but in her place he had conjured up a very unsubstantial creation and endowed it with every virtue that he could find a name for—a creation with pale golden hair and languishing smile, and pink-and-white complexion and drooping figure.

And now this dream of his, like many of his youthful hopes and ambitions, was lying crushed and dead. It was another of the little ironies of life. Before the fruit had time to form the blossom fell. The day had not time to break before the night came on.

At length he espied Nathan and his father coming hurriedly towards him, each carrying a coil of rope slung over his shoulder. And quickly following these were a number of others with ladders and lanterns, and such other things as might be needed in case of accident.

They came very silently across the fields, no one exchanging a word with his neighbour. Behind St. Iago tower a great round moon was rising slowly, as if to watch over the operations, while in the valley a white mist was stretching out its hands in all directions and creeping ghost-like up the sides of the hills.

In a few minutes Justin found himself surrounded by a dozen of his neighbours. To fling two or three ladders across the wide mouth of the shaft was the work of a very short time; then, tying a lighted lantern to the end of a rope, he crept out on this somewhat insecure platform until he found himself over the centre of the pit.

Lying on his face, and looking intently between the staves of the ladder down into the darkness, he began slowly to lower the lantern. His heart was beating uncomfortably fast. His breath came and went in gasps. Around him stood a circle of men, no one speaking. The very corncrakes had ceased to call.

Down and down into the darkness the lighted lantern sank. How oppressive the silence was! He wished that Nathan or his father would talk, but they were too interested in seeing the rope paid out.

Still down and down. How cruelly deep the shaft was! It was no wonder no answering voice had come in response to his call. A drop to the bottom would mean instant death.

Ah, the lantern had struck against something and was heeling over on its side—something soft also. He raised it a little and dropped it again. What was it? The light was too feeble and far away to see anything clearly.

"Can you see anything, Justin?" called John Pentyre from the bank.

"Yes; there is something at the bottom," he replied, "but I cannot make out clearly what. Something light-coloured and soft."

"It's the maid, no doubt," Nathan answered, with a little gasp.

"Is any one there?" Justin called down into the echoing pit, and every one held his breath and listened, but no answer came up through the darkness.

"It's no use shouting to dead people," called Nathan from the bank.

Justin made the rope fast and then crept back to the bank. Instantly the others crowded round him.

"Well, Justin, what's to be done now?" his father asked.

"Some one must go down," was the reply.

"Easier said than done, my boy. If we had a windlass and kibble there'd be no difficulty."

"There'll be no difficulty as it is," was the answer. "Let's knot the other rope. We know the depth now. That's it, Nathan; let the knots be eight or ten feet apart. Now get the other ladder and throw it across the shaft in the other direction. That's it, men; you see it's a couple

of feet above the other ladders. Now make fast
the rope to it, and let it drop between the lower
ladders."

The men obeyed his instructions without a
word and with the utmost alacrity. In a few
minutes the knotted rope was made fast to the
upper and transverse ladder. Justin watched the
operation with the keenest interest. His life
might depend upon a knot.

At length the rope was as fast as it could
be made, and, divesting himself of his coat, and
fastening a lighted candle to his bowler hat by
means of a lump of clay, he crept cautiously out
on the lower ladders till he came to the spot
where the rope dangled between them. Looking
down, he saw that the lantern was still alight,
but it revealed nothing to his anxious eyes.

"We shall soon know the best or worst now,"
he said, as he grasped the rope.

"May the Lord preserve thee, my son," John
Pentyre said, fervently.

"Amen," cried Nathan and several of the
others.

And when they looked again, Justin had
disappeared into the gaping abyss.

"WE SHALL SOON KNOW THE BEST OR WORST NOW."

P. 62.

CHAPTER VI

HOW IT HAPPENED

> "Our eyes are holden : and we may not see
> What lies before us."

WHEN Ruby started out for her afternoon's walk she had not the remotest idea of running into danger. She was getting used to the country and beginning to enjoy it. At first its very silence somewhat oppressed her. She had been so accustomed to the life, and movement, and colour of London streets and parks, that the absence of people and the absence of noise impressed her with a curious sense of forlornness and solitude.

But after a week at Endilloe this feeling had worn away entirely. What at first had seemed a solemn and unpeopled landscape was now a vast hive of life—not human life—but life in such forms as hitherto she had been quite unaccustomed to. There was not a hedgerow or pool, or bank of furze or heather; not a stream or copse, or stretch of moorland that was not, in its way, a new revelation. Even the clouds took new shapes to what they did in the city, and the wind sang with new voices and in sweeter tones, while the sunsets were glorious beyond all that she had imagined.

And then, transcending everything else was the ever-changing sea. She became more and more fascinated by it every day. It was so solemn, so vast, so mighty. It spoke in such deep, mysterious tones; it seemed to hush all querulous voices and banish all trivial thoughts. She could not be frivolous in its presence, or heedless, or flippant. If there was any latent greatness in her nature it seemed to touch it into life. It made her serious and thoughtful, but never sad.

As yet she had seen it only in its gentlest moods. Its anger and cruelty she had not witnessed. When she stood on the cliffs or walked sedately at low tide, along its beach of hard, yellow sand, the sunshine lay upon it, and its translucent depths caught a dozen hues that she had no name for. Some day she would see it in its anger and fury, then it would stir other feelings in her heart.

She meant, when she left the house, to go for a walk along the banks of the river, in the shade of the alders and willows. But she had not been out of doors many minutes when the sea seemed to call her from over the low-browed hill. So she took a field-path that led to the Downs, and thence to the cliffs.

She was in a very meditative mood and not disposed to hurry in the least. This great, solemn, open country, so hushed and peaceful, with scarcely a sound to disturb its quiet and repose, seemed to hold in check her natural impetuosity. She did not want to run and skip. Her mood caught the tone of her surroundings. There were so many things to arrest her attention—now a butterfly, now a bird, and now a rare kind of flower growing unheeded by the roadside—that she wanted to be quiet and move leisurely, and think her highest and holiest thoughts.

The path she took led through a small field planted with green crops. Amos Blue, a hired man, was busy hoeing turnips, but catching a glimpse of Ruby's white gown as she got over the stile, he straightened his back and, leaning on his hoe, waited for her to come up. Amos was a man without pride and without prejudices. He did not despise the dwellers in cities as Nathan Hendy did. But perhaps the reason for that was to be found in the fact that he had a son, and an only son, somewhere in the great world of London. Hence any one from that

far-off city had always a certain interest for
Amos. They might, in some way, have come
into contact with his boy Dan'l.

How Dan'l got to London was a problem
that no one pretended to solve. He left St.
Iago three or four years previously in search
of work. For nine months nothing was heard
of him. Then the village postman brought a
letter to Amos bearing the London postmark,
since which time three other letters had come
which left Amos's soul exceedingly hungry, for
Dan'l, with curious reticence, said almost nothing
about himself or about his work. In fact, he
gave no hint as to whether, in the struggle of
life, he was failing or succeeding. Each letter
began in the same way :—

"Dear father and mother,—I writes you these
few lines, hopin' they will find you in good
'ealth as they leaves me at present."

What followed was really of no importance
to any one. In his first letter he did condescend
to say that London was a terrible big place,
which piece of information had often set Amos
wondering as to the relative sizes of London
and St. Iago Churchtown. Amos was not an
imaginative man, and never having gone beyond
the bounds of his own parish, he could not easily
conceive that St. Iago Churchtown could be
much outdone in the matter of population.

Nevertheless, such mind as Amos had was truly athirst for knowledge, and he never lost an opportunity for making inquiries of people who might possibly know more than he knew himself. The great drawback from which Amos suffered was, he forgot so fast. Indeed, his power of forgetting was phenomenal.

When he saw the flutter of Ruby's white dress on the stile he reflected: "That's the little maid from London, I'll be bound." And, true to his instinct, he prepared himself to gather what information he could.

When Ruby drew sufficiently near Amos turned himself round, and said—

"Good afternoon, miss. You couldn't tell me the time of day now, could 'ee?"

"Oh yes, I can!" Ruby said, brightly. "It's just a quarter-past three."

"Oh, 'tes, es it? I thank'ee all the same. I reckon you be the little maid from London?"

"Yes, I am from London," Ruby answered, an amused smile lighting up her sweet oval face.

"Iss, so I reckon. I s'pose London es a terrible big plaace? Our Dan'l said in wan of his letters as 't was terrible big. I s'pose you don't know our Dan'l?"

"No; I don't think I have the pleasure," Ruby answered, still smiling.

"I thought p'raps you might 'ave seed'n lately. It's a longish time since he wrot'."

"No; I'm not aware that I've seen him."

"Thought p'raps you might, as he's been livin' up long there—'bout three years now. He's a tallish chap, is our Dan'l, with red 'air, an' terrible muffly 'bout his face'n 'ands."

"But he wouldn't wear a muffler this warm weather?" Ruby questioned.

"What ded'ee say now?" Amos questioned, drawing himself up. "I ded'n say nawthin' 'bout no muffler. I said he was terrible muffly. You know, he 'ad muffles (freckles) all over 'is face'n 'ands."

"I'm afraid I don't quite understand you," Ruby said, with a look of perplexity in her eyes.

"Why, surely," Amos said, pityingly, "you don't main to say you be that ignorant you don't knaw what muffles is?"

"I'm afraid I must plead guilty to that charge," she said, laughing.

"Oh dear, now. And ded'n your father never send you to no school, then?"

"Oh yes, I went to school when I was younger."

"Then p'raps you're like me, a terrible power of forgettin'?"

"Do you forget easily?"

"Oah, terrible aisy, miss. It's no sooner

come than it's gone like. Susan do say as I've forgotten more'n I ever larned. But about London, miss. Es it much biggern St. Iago Churchtown now?"

"Oh yes, very much bigger."

"That's what everybody do say now. Iss, everybody do say the same. I've thought lots 'bout it lately. An' I've said to Susan, I 'ave— Susan's my missus, you knaw—I've said to Susan. 'Susan,' says I, 'I expect if I was to go up to London Station and ax for our Dan'l nobody'd be able to tell me where he lived.' Now what do you think of it, miss?"

"Well, I am inclined to think that that would not be the surest way of finding Daniel," Ruby answered, trying her best to keep her face straight.

"Iss, that's what I do say to Susan. But thank'ee all the same, miss," and Amos turned once more to his hoeing.

Ruby jumped lightly over the stile at the far end of the turnip-field; crossed another field in which a number of cows were feeding, and then made a bee line across the common for the sea.

Passing close to the big mound of rubbish that surrounded the shaft already spoken of, some rapidly ripening blackberries caught her eye. Running lightly up the bank, her quick eye took in the situation in a moment. The depth of the shaft, however, did not trouble her. One or two quite ripe blackberries were a yard away, so, pulling off her gloves, and dropping one in attempting to push them into her pocket, she trampled down the nearest brambles, and reached out her white hand and plucked the humble fruit. It was the work of a minute; then she ran lightly down the bank again, leaving her white glove behind her.

It was an unfortunate thing, for it put her searchers on the wrong track, and wasted much precious time.

In a few minutes she was on the cliffs, in sight of the great sea which she had learnt to love. The tide was low and was still receding. For awhile she sat on a bank of heather and listened to its low music. Then she decided she would go down to the beach. There was no danger with reasonable care. A good path led by a number of zig-zags. She had been down a number of times already. Why should she not go again?

The long line of cliffs was quite deserted; not a soul was to be seen in any direction. She could see for a mile along the hard, yellow sand, and no shadow fell upon it; but the tripper's season had not commenced; moreover, the En-dilloe cliffs were out of his beat.

Had Ruby lived longer by the sea she might

have exercised more caution. It is never wise to make excursions on the cliffs alone. There are so many little risks that the stranger does not think of.

In the present case it was only a loose stone that twisted Ruby's ankle when two-thirds the way down. It was so sudden and unexpected that she had no time to save herself. With a sudden cry she fell over the side of the path and struck a ledge of rock four or five feet lower down, rolled off that to a lower ledge still, and so down and down till she lay upon the hard, yellow sand, bruised, and bleeding, and unconscious.

The hours of the afternoon wore away and the sun went down, and still she lay there without moving and without regaining consciousness. On the one side rose the beetling cliffs, which prevented any one from above seeing her, and on the other side stretched the moaning sea, which came nearer and nearer as the daylight vanished into the darkness.

Nathan Hendy came out on the cliffs and strained his eyes along the beach and shouted till he was hoarse, but no voice came to him in reply, and she was too far under the cliff for him to see her.

And still the tide came crawling in and the darkness grew deeper, till the great round moon rose over the cliffs and looked down upon the still, unconscious figure. Then the sea seemed to catch sight of her, and the waves ran laughing up the beach and looked at her for a moment and then back again. Then other and bolder waves drew nearer still, and almost touched her cheek, then hurried back to tell the rest. Then a rude wave came up and kissed her lips and shouted in her ear, and threw sand into her shining hair.

Ah, the sea had always seemed to her kind and gentle, but it had no pity now.

CHAPTER VII

AHOY !

> " Life wears another face
> When love awakes."

Spite of the law of gravitation, Justin climbed the rope much more rapidly than he descended it. A dead sheep, which he found at the bottom of the shaft, was not particularly agreeable company. And, satisfying himself that nothing else that ever possessed life was there, he hurried up the rope, hand over hand, with an alacrity that was an astonishment to himself.

He was fairly well exhausted by the time he pulled himself up between the two ladders, and for awhile he sat quite still and breathed hard.

He had answered from the bottom the one question that had been shouted to him, and now his companions stood round him in a circle and waited for him to speak. When he had recovered his breath, he crept along the ladder until he reached *terra firma*, then he walked

73

slowly down the bank, and was quickly followed by his father and all the others.

Nathan broke the silence. Nathan was quite indignant that so much labour and effort had been spent for nothing.

"What can 'ee expect of people brought up in sich a way?" he said, in a tone of scorn; and he walked two or three paces towards Endilloe by way of emphasizing his remark.

"It is possible she may still be alive," Justin said, without heeding Nathan. "Amos Blue saw her in the turnip-field, going towards the river."

"But we've searched the river already," said John Pentyre.

"Not thoroughly," Justin answered. "Go as far as Tregarrick Wood. I'll follow as soon as I'm rested a bit."

He was the youngest man of the lot, and yet they obeyed him. Some men are born to command—they do it unconsciously, and with no thought of assuming any kind of dictatorship. Others obey, and without resentment, glad of a will that is stronger than theirs, and of a purpose that does not waver.

In a few minutes Justin found himself quite alone. He saw the others vanishing like spectres in the dim moonlight. For a few minutes he sat on the bank, and rested his face in his hands. How strangely this unseen girl was dominating his thoughts—his very life! How completely she absorbed all his interests.

Suddenly he rose to his feet, and put his hand to his mouth, as though to shout to his companions, then he thought better of it.

"One is as good as ten," he said to himself. "I'll go alone. Dorothy says she is passionately fond of the sea." And he turned and strode rapidly up the hillside.

In a few minutes he was standing on the cliff looking down at the incoming tide, that raced and rippled in the moonlight with a sound that was full of music. The long strip of beach that was still uncovered lay in deep shadow. It would not be high water for more than a hour yet.

After standing for awhile looking and listening, he commenced to descend the very path that Ruby had descended earlier in the day. He threaded his way with caution, for he knew what one false step might mean. Down, and still down, the easy zig-zag, then he paused suddenly, and put his hand to his ear and listened.

*   *   *   *   *

Meanwhile a larger wave than usual had splashed its cold salt water all over Ruby's face. It seemed a cruel, hungry wave, but in reality it was kind; it awoke her from the long trance in which she had lain, and restored her once more to consciousness. With a little cry, she sat up, and stared wonderingly around her. For several minutes she was unable to realize who she was, or where she was, or what had happened, and all the while the waves kept crawling in and in, soaking her pretty white dress, and chilling her almost to the bone.

At length, as in a sudden flash, everything came back to her, and with another cry she tried to struggle to her feet; but she dropped back again with a bitter moan of pain; she was too hurt to move without the most excruciating torture, and yet to sit still would simply be to drown by slow inches. Every moment the tide came in further and further. How cruel it seemed to her now, as it sucked away the sand on which she sat, and mocked her in her misery.

She was too terror-stricken to lose consciousness again. Every faculty of the mind was preternaturally active. She thought of the mental agony of her mother, of the distress of the Pentyres, of the sorrow of her father when he returned from London.

"Oh, I cannot die here like this, by slow inches!" she said to herself. "Oh, it is horrible —horrible!" and she screamed aloud for help in her terror.

It was this cry that arrested Justin's attention, as he came cautiously down the cliff-path; the next moment the cry was repeated, and with a shout: "I'm coming!" he hurried down the remaining distance at a break-neck pace, flinging caution to the winds, and coming within an ace of destruction more than once.

In an incredibly short time he was at the foot of the cliffs, looking eagerly right and left; then another faint cry for help drew his eyes in the right direction. A long way out beyond the edge of the tide, it seemed to him, the head and shoulders of some one rose dimly above the water.

With another shout: "I'm coming!" he splashed into the creeping waves, and in a moment he was by her side.

"You are Ruby Loveday?" he questioned, stooping down and gathering her up in his strong arms.

"Yes; we are staying at Endilloe. Do you think you can save me?"

"I can try, at any rate," he said, with a laugh. "Are you much hurt?"

"I'm afraid I am a good deal. I was unable to move from where I was."

"It's lucky I found you," he said, making a strong effort to keep his voice steady. "We've been searching for you for hours, and had almost given you up as lost."

He had begun to ascend the cliff-path by this time, and he soon found, strong as he was, that he was not carrying a child.

"I must ask you to clasp your arms about my neck, if you have strength to do so," he said, a curious thrill running through him as he did so.

She answered him by doing as he told her. The situation was not without its touch of romance. Her head, with its wealth of dripping hair, rested on his shoulder; her cheek was close to his. He could feel her breath upon his neck, as he climbed higher and higher; and it seemed to put new strength into him.

Now and then a groan of pain escaped her lips, and he felt instinctively how resolutely she was trying to keep still. He made no attempt to look at her. He could not if he tried. Her face was too close to his.

Occasionally, when the pain was not so severe, she could not help wondering who he was. She had caught more than one glimpse of his face in the moonlight, and he seemed to her to be a very handsome man. And then how strong he was! She seemed but a mere child in his arms.

Halfway up the cliff he sat down on a ledge

of rock and rested himself. She did not remove her head from his shoulder, nor her arms from about his neck.

"I fear you are in great pain," he said, with a ring of genuine sympathy in his voice.

"I am at times," she answered. "I'm afraid my left foot is smashed all to pieces."

"I hope it is not so bad as that," he said; "but we shall soon be home now."

"Do you live near here?" she questioned.

"At Endilloe. I am Justin Pentyre."

"Oh, I am so glad! Dorothy has often spoken of you. But you are nothing like I pictured you."

"No?"

She did not reply until they got to the top of the cliff. Then she said—

"How strong you are! Oh, I shall never be able to thank you enough as long as I live!"

"Don't try," he said. "I don't want any thanks; to have saved you is reward enough."

And he hurried across the strip of common, and was soon in the fir-plantation. Here he had to thread his way with care, on account of Ruby's damaged foot; but, thanks to the great round moon, that was now shining in all her splendour, he found no difficulty. He was half disposed to raise a shout, when he got out on the Endilloe side; but, on second thoughts, he decided to carry Ruby all the way, and keep all the glory of it to himself.

"How distressed mother will be to see me in this plight!" Ruby said, as they descended the field towards the orchard.

"She will forget everything in her gladness at seeing you alive."

"Yes, so she will;" and then he felt scalding tears running down his neck.

For a moment these tears quite unmanned him. He felt weak and nerveless. He wanted to sit down and rest. Then he was seized with a passionate desire to raise her face and kiss away her tears, and comfort her as her mother might.

He quickly recovered himself, however. He remembered her position and his own. She was the only daughter of a wealthy London merchant, and he was a salesman in a village store.

"I'd better not spoil everything by making a fool of myself at the beginning," he reflected; and he pushed open the orchard gate with his foot.

By this time every nerve in his body was tingling with excitement. The lost was found, and he alone knew of it. He was the bringer of good tidings. He could not contain himself any longer, and he raised a great shout: "Ahoy! Ahoy! Ahoy!"

In a moment three women came rushing out of the house—Dorothy and the two mothers.

"Is that you, Justin?" Dorothy cried.

"Aye. I've found her," he shouted. "She's here alive. "Ahoy! Ahoy!""

And the shout was taken up in the distant fields: "Ahoy! Ahoy!" And the night-wind carried the cry into Tregarrick Wood, and the searchers turned rightabout-face, and responded with the same thrilling cry: "Ahoy! Ahoy!" for they knew what it meant; and in a few moments the thud of running feet was borne in from the distant fields, and middle-aged men leaped hedges with an agility they had not shown since they were young.

In the meanwhile Mrs. Loveday had cried for a few moments on Ruby's neck; then she led the way into the house.

Justin still bore his burden bravely, though he was all but spent. Through the big kitchen he followed the women, along the passage, and into the Lovedays' room.

Ruby was in a state of collapse when he laid her down on the big sofa, and for several minutes she appeared to be in a dead faint. Justin sank back into an easy-chair, and gripped the elbows with his hands, for a thin mist had come up before his eyes, and the room seemed to be spinning round like a whirligig at a fair.

No one, however, took any notice of him. Every eye in the room but his was fixed on Ruby. She looked a strangely bedraggled nymph as she lay there on the sofa. Her hair was tangled and dripping. Her dress was soaked with the sea-water, and clung tightly to her figure. Sea-sand was all over her, on her eyebrows and in her ears. Her lips were tightly shut, her face was as white as the dead.

Dorothy stood by chafing her cold hands, and Mrs. Loveday was doing her best to get some brandy between her teeth. In the meanwhile the hum of voices and the clatter of hob-nailed shoes were heard in the kitchen. A dozen voices appeared to be asking the same question at the same time, and Mrs. Pentyre was doing her best to explain matters.

Justin, in his easy-chair, heard like one who is only half-awake. He had no desire to rouse himself, or to take any further part. The reaction had set in. He was more completely spent than ever he had been before in his life. He heard his father give orders to Nathan to ride across to St. Iago Churchtown, and fetch Dr. Morrison at once, and he tried to rouse himself to say he would go. But the effort was too great.

Then he heard Mrs. Loveday say, with a thrill of joy in her voice, "She is coming round at last. We must get her upstairs and into bed as quickly as possible."

"Justin will carry her upstairs," Dorothy said, quickly, and she turned at once and looked at her brother.

The next moment she was kneeling by his side.

"Are you not well, Justin?" she said, anxiously.

"Oh yes, I'm all right," he said, trying to smile; "just a little spent, that is all. Fetch me a glass of water, will you, and I shall be all right."

"Drink this," said Mrs. Loveday, coming forward.

And Justin drank it, not knowing what it was, and in a few minutes the mist cleared away from his eyes, and the spinning room slowed down, and at length stood still.

"Now I shall see her face," was his thought. "I wonder if she is anything like I pictured her?"

CHAPTER VIII

MAN'S EXTREMITY

"We do our best, and wait :
The issue rests with God."

RUBY's dishevelled condition seemed rather to add to her charm than detract from it. She was one of those dainty creatures that look pretty under any circumstances. Her face was such a perfect oval, her features so delicately cut, her complexion so clear, her eyes so large and expressive, and her smile so sweet and radiant, that if she were only a flower-seller in the street people would be sure to turn and look at her a second time.

Justin rose from his chair and looked at her with an expression of wonder in his eyes. The light of the lamp fell full upon her face, and lit up her large, expressive eyes. She was not a bit like the Ruby of his imagination. The tall, fair, languid beauty, with golden hair and pink-and-white complexion, might exist somewhere, but her name was not Ruby Loveday. This brown-haired maiden was of quite another type.

She greeted him with one of her sweetest smiles.

"I am sorry to have to trouble you again," she said; "but would you mind carrying me upstairs to my room?—you are so strong."

He had felt weak enough a moment before; but such an appeal would give a giant's strength to a much feebler man than he. He saw that she was fighting pain and weakness with desperate energy. She wore a smile upon her face when it would have been a relief to her to have shrieked.

"I fear it will give you great pain to move you," he said, sympathetically.

"I know it will," she said, with the same sweet smile playing about her lips; "but it has to be borne, and I must make the best of it."

He did not speak again, but bent over her at once. She stretched out her hands and clasped him about the neck as she had done before. Very gently and tenderly he gathered her up in his arms. All his strength came back to him with a rush. She seemed but as a child.

Dorothy went before with a light, and Mrs. Loveday followed. Poor Ruby cried out more than once as Justin slowly climbed the stairs; but he reached the top at length, and went

forward into Ruby's room. Without a word,
he laid her on the low bed, and turned away.
There was a singing in his ears again, and his
heart was beating at fever speed.

Down in the big kitchen a dozen men were
waiting for him, eager to hear the story he had
to tell.   But he was in no humour for conversation.   He wanted to be alone, so that he
might commune with his own heart.   Nevertheless, he did his best to satisfy the natural
curiosity of his neighbours.

"But why did 'ee send us oal waun way
while you went the t'other?" asked a keen-eyed
little man, William Sparrow by name.

"I don't know," Justin answered, indifferently.
"It was just a sudden impulse, that is all."

"And do you think she is much hurt?" his
father asked.

"I am afraid she is," was the answer.   "You
see, she lay for hours quite unconscious, and
that means more than a hurt foot."

"She seems a terrible plucky little maid,"
said an old farmer, after emptying his mouth
of a cloud of tobacco smoke.

"You are right," said Justin, with sudden
energy; "she is plucky.   But here comes the
doctor, I fancy.   We shall know soon the extent
of her injuries."

For the next half-hour the old eight-day clock

could be heard very distinctly in the room.
All attempts at conversation ended in failure.
John Pentyre fetched out his tobacco-jar, and
a handful of clay pipes for those who smoked;
the others sat round in all manner of attitudes
and stared at nothing in particular.

Every now and then some one turned his
head and looked at the clock : the minutes
travelled by slowly. Mrs. Pentyre came into
the room at length, and went to the stove to
get some hot water. She looked very grave,
and her eyes were wet, as though she had been
crying.

"Well, mother," said John Pentyre, "how is
the little maid going on ? "

"I hardly know," was the hesitating reply.
"I'm afraid she's a great deal more hurt than
any of us think."

"Does Dr. Morrison say so ? "

"He says nothing, but he looks very grave,
and he hinted just now that her foot was not the
worst part of her injuries."

Justin looked up eagerly, but he did not ask
any questions; and Mrs. Pentyre immediately
after left the room, closing the door behind
her.

Then the tick of the old clock filled the room
again, for no one was in the humour to dispute
its right to be heard.

At length, after what seemed an unconscionably long time, the doctor's heavy footsteps sounded on the stairs, and John and Justin rose at once, and went out into the hall to intercept him.

They came back again five minutes later, looking very grave. The others stood up, and waited for the verdict.

Justin replied at once to their inquiring looks. "The doctor declines to give any very definite opinion at present. He admits that her injuries are serious, but how serious he cannot tell yet. He will be better able to judge to-morrow morning."

The little company melted rapidly away after that. Some said good night, or what was intended for "good night," for, generally speaking, the word "good" was treated as being entirely superfluous; others stole out into the summer moonlight without speaking.

John filled his pipe again when his neighbours had left him, but Justin stole wearily and dejectedly off to bed. For a long time he lay with strained attention, listening for every sound. Once or twice he fancied he heard a low moan of pain, and the sound shot through him like a knife. He wondered why it was that he was so troubled and anxious. Had it been Dorothy herself who lay ill, he could not have been more concerned. This Ruby Loveday was nothing to him——

But, stop. The events of that evening had changed everything. He had saved her life, and by that act he had created a right——

But what right?

Well, the right to be interested in her. She could never be again as a stranger to him. That which you save is, in a measure, yours. He had established a claim which he would not insist upon, though he could never forget its existence.

He fell asleep at length, and for seven hours slept the sleep of utter weariness and exhaustion; and when he woke next morning to the chirruping of innumerable birds he felt little if any the worse for the experiences of the previous night.

Dorothy did not put in an appearance at breakfast. She had been up all night, and was now taking a little rest. Mrs. Pentyre could say little that was favourable respecting the patient. In fact, she seemed in great pain, and considerably more feverish than on the previous night.

Justin went off to Trelford with a heavy heart. He was beginning to be afraid that he had only saved Ruby from death in one form that she might meet it in another.

When he got back in the evening he found that Mr. Loveday had just returned from

London, and that Ruby had brightened up considerably directly he came into the room, and that she seemed much better than earlier in the day.

This was satisfactory news, and Justin ate his supper with a much better appetite than he had shown at breakfast.

But the days that followed were days of great anxiety and of gradually lessening hope. Each morning the news from the sick-room seemed less promising than on the previous morning. The patient was bright and cheerful, and talked of getting better directly; but those who kept watch by her saw that she got gradually weaker, and that the hope of recovery was vanishing farther and farther into the distance.

Justin was consumed with a longing he could not understand to see her; yet no one ever suggested such a thing, and he had not the courage to ask. He envied Dorothy the privilege of being so constantly by her side, and was too proud to admit by word or look that his anxiety was becoming almost too painful to be borne.

Mr. Loveday talked no more about business. It was mainly for his child that he toiled from year to year, and added to his already ample fortune. But now that she seemed slipping from his grasp business was nothing. All his life seemed wrapped up in Ruby.

Each morning and afternoon he went out for a short walk; the rest of his time he spent in the sick-room. He did not say much, but he watched every change in the invalid with an eagerness that was almost painful.

On the fourth day a specialist was called in from Plymouth, and on the sixth day the Lovedays' family doctor journeyed down from London; but to the onlookers it seemed as if nothing could save her. The doctors said very little, and that little was anything but of a hopeful character.

Mr. Loveday was very reticent, but it was evident that he was preparing for the worst. On the tenth day the whisper ran through the house, and found its way out into the fields, and was carried across the valley to St. Iago Churchtown, that "the doctors could do no more for the little maid from London; that the issue now was in the hands of Providence."

It was early-closing day, and Justin had hurried home with the speed of the wind. Dorothy met him at the door, and told him what the doctors had said. For a moment he looked at her as if about to ask a question, then he turned away, and wandered down across the fields.

It was a beautiful, sunshiny day, with a cool, pleasant wind blowing in from the sea. All around him the cornfields were yellowing in the summer sun, and the air was steeped with the odours of the fields and pine-wood. But for Justin there was no sunshine and no fragrance.

Had any one predicted three weeks before what he was now passing through he would have laughed at the suggestion. He had made up his mind to dislike the Lovedays and all their ways; yet now he felt he would willingly die himself, if by that means he could save Ruby's life.

In one of the fields he came upon Amos Blue.

"An' 'ow be the little maid?" Amos asked, stretching his back, and looking inquiringly at Justin.

"Very ill, Amos—very ill. The doctors can do no more."

"Is that so, now?" Amos said, dropping his eyes. "Is that so? Then, what is to be done, Mr. Justin?"

"Nothing can be done, Amos," Justin answered, a little bitterly, "except leave her in the hands of Providence."

"An' be you goin' to do that?" Amos questioned, with the faintest suggestion of a smile upon his weather-beaten face. " Be the doctors goin' to leave her there ? "

" Well, I suppose so. There is nothing else they can do."

" Ah ! well, then, there may be a chance for the little maid now ; " and Amos smiled quite broadly.

" What do you mean, Amos ? "

" I main, Mr. Justin, that man's extremity es God's opportunity. Have 'ee forgot that, Mr. Justin ? You've oal been trustin' in the doctors afore, now you be agoin' to trust in the Lord. An' I do say that there's a chance now for the little maid. When men fail, then the Almighty comes in ; " and Amos turned to his work again.

Justin looked up, and saw Dorothy hurrying across the field towards him.

CHAPTER IX

AKIN TO PAIN

" Pleasures are like poppies spread,
    You seize the flower, its bloom is shed."

A MONTH later Justin had entered into a new
experience, and an experience that in all his
dreams and imaginings he had never contemplated or deemed possible.   It came to him as a
painful shock which, for awhile, seemed to shift
the very centre of gravity and made him
uncertain of himself and everything else.

That Ruby was unwittingly the cause of this
may be readily guessed.   Ruby persisted in
living, in spite of the fact that Dr. Morrison gave
up her case as hopeless.   When the tide of her
life had ebbed out to its furthest limit, and
Dorothy rushed off into the fields, blinded and
choking with grief, to tell Justin that the very
worst had come, Ruby looked up and smiled,
then fell into a sweet, refreshing sleep, from
which she awoke several hours later and declared
to her mother that she felt ever so much better,

and that she thought she would be able to get up on the following day.   She did not, however, get up the next day nor the next week, but within a month she was well enough to be carried downstairs, and to receive visitors.   Justin was the first of these to be admitted into her pre-sence—and he was not a little elated at the favour shown to him.

Dorothy met him at the end of the lane one Thursday afternoon on his return from Trelford.

"Go and make yourself presentable, Justin," she said, " for Ruby wants to see you."

"Wants to see me?" he questioned, for Dorothy's announcement had so taken him by surprise that he had nothing better to say at the moment.

"She has spoken about you lots of times lately, and said how thankful she felt," Dorothy went on, "but I fancy she wants just to tell you herself——"

" I hope she does not want to do anything of the kind," he interrupted.   "I shall just make an ass of myself if she begins to thank me."

"Not since you know beforehand," Dorothy said with a smile.   "And, after all, it is the most natural thing in the world that she should want to see you."

"Yes, I suppose so," he said, absently ; for he remembered how for weeks he had been literally pining for just a glimpse of her face, and how he had listened constantly in the hall, hoping that some tone of her voice would float down the stairs to him.

"You had better put on your coat of mail," Dorothy said, banteringly, "for I really think she looks prettier than ever."

"Indeed! I thought you told me she had wasted to a shadow."

"Oh, that was weeks ago. She looks pale still, of course, but that is scarcely any drawback."

Justin walked slowly into the house, and retired at once to his own room. He had played his part before Dorothy remarkably well, and she had no idea how intensely excited he was.

At first he was disposed to dress himself in his Sunday best, but thought better of it.

"I'll go just as I am," he said to himself. "What can it matter? She knows I go to Trelford every day. Besides——"

But he did not finish the sentence. His heart was in a tumult, and he was half angry with himself that it should be so.

Dorothy was waiting for him at the foot of the stairs, to conduct him to the Loveday apartments.

"Why, you have not donned your best after all," she said, inquiringly.

"No."

"I thought you were making a most elaborate toilet, by the time you've been."

"Then you are mistaken for once."

"Don't you wish to see her?"

"I don't want to be thanked, at any rate."

"Oh, if that's all, you'll soon get over it."

"I hope so."

She darted an inquiring glance at him, then led the way out of the room. Whether Justin was absolutely indifferent, or whether it was all put on, was a point she was not quite able to decide.

Ruby was waiting for her visitor without trepidation and without even curiosity. She felt no interest in Justin except in so far as he had rescued her from an awkward and dangerous situation. For this, of course, she was grateful— exceedingly grateful. She had nearly forgotten what he was like. She had a vague recollection that he was tall, muscular, and rather good-looking, with a strong, resolute face and kind-looking eyes. But he was out of her world completely. He was only the son of a farmer, and served in a shop for a less salary than her father paid his gardener.

Nevertheless, he had saved her life, and she felt grateful, and wanted to tell him so, and when she had done that she would have done her duty, and there would be an end of it.

Dorothy was quite right when she said that Ruby looked lovelier than ever. Reclining on a roomy old sofa, well bolstered up with cushions, and attired in a gown of most becoming make and material, she made as pretty a picture as one could wish to see. The afternoon's sunshine filled the room with a soft, warm light, and tinged Ruby's cheeks with the faintest suggestion of colour.

Justin caught his breath when he came into her presence. The reality outdistanced far and away all his fancies. He often wondered afterwards what she was dressed in, but he could never describe a single detail. Dresses at Endilloe were made for wear and not for artistic effect—that was but a secondary consideration. Ruby's dress might be of very little use in a farmhouse; from an utilitarian point of view it would be an utter failure, but as a work of art, as a study in neutral tints, as a setting for natural beauty of no common order, nothing could have been better.

Justin advanced shyly and somewhat awkwardly, and when she held out her hand to him, he was almost afraid to take it in his lest it should crumble up in his grasp—it looked so white, and small, and fragile.

"I am glad you have come," she said, in her bright, frank way. "I have wanted to see you for days."

Justin could have said truthfully that he had been pining to see her for weeks, but he wisely kept silent on that point, and simply answered that he was glad she was able to get downstairs again.

"I little thought when you carried me upstairs that night," she replied, "that I should have been kept a prisoner so long."

"I think we, none of us, imagined you were so seriously hurt——"

"But I'm nearly all right again now," she interrupted, brightly. "Won't you sit down? You are not driven for time, I hope?"

"Oh no; I have nothing to do," he said colouring slightly, and dropping somewhat awkwardly into the chair she indicated.

She saw in a moment that he was nervous, and so exerted herself to place him at his ease. Dorothy having seen him to the door, had retired to an adjoining room to talk to Mrs. Loveday. Mr. Loveday was in London again, looking after his business.

"Do you know, I'm pining to get out-of-doors again," she said, glancing towards the window. "I'm half afraid this fine weather will give out before I've a chance to enjoy it."

"I don't think it will," he answered. "We often get lovely weather right into October."

"I hope it will be so this year. What a holiday I've had, haven't I? Think of it. I'm really ashamed of myself for having spoilt everybody's pleasure."

"But your getting better makes amends for everything," he said, bluntly.

"It's kind of you to say that," she said, looking at him with frank, smiling eyes. "You have all been so good to me. I shall have to get used to the idea of being permanently in debt."

"Is the thought an unpleasant one?"

"Oh no, not in the least. It might not be pleasant to be in some people's debt, for they might make themselves nasty over it. But everybody at Endilloe is so genuinely kind that the idea of going away in your debt is rather pleasant than otherwise."

"We shall all feel sorry when you go," he said, after a pause.

"Do you really mean that?" she asked, with a little laugh.

"I do, indeed. We shall miss you awfully."

"But you have scarcely ever seen me, or any of us, in fact."

"But we have grown used to you being in the house," he answered, colouring. "You have created a new interest, if you will allow me to say so. Why, even Nathan and Amos will feel lost when they can no longer inquire at the house how you are."

"Is Amos the man with the son in London?"

"The same."

"Oh, then, I like him. He's nature unadorned. Don't you think so?"

"Well, yes. There's not much adornment about Amos."

"He quite pitied me because I did not know what 'muffles' were, and wanted to know if my father had never sent me to school. Dorothy and I have laughed over it till we have ached."

"He would mean no disrespect," he answered, quickly.

"Oh, I know that. That's why I like him so much. He is so simple, sincere, and transparent. I wish I could imitate his manners. I shall have some further conversation with him when I am able to get out."

"Nothing will delight him more. Did Dorothy tell you what he said when the doctor had given you up?"

"No; what did he say?"

"I told him the doctors had done their utmost, and left you in the hands of Providence. 'Is it come to that?' he questioned. I told him it had. And you should have seen his face brighten. 'Now, Mr. Justin,' he said, 'there's a chance for the little maid. Man's extremity is God's opportunity,' and he turned to his work quite cheerfully."

Ruby did not reply, but a far-away look came into her eyes, as though she saw something far beyond the bounds of the room.

Justin watched her with a strange tumult in his heart. He knew well enough that this brown-haired, sweet-voiced maiden was all the world to him, and yet, had she dwelt in another planet, she could not have been further removed. It was one of the ironies of life that he should fall in love with one so completely out of his sphere, and after all his protestations, too.

Fate seemed to be persistently unkind to the Pentyres. They had been robbed of their inheritance, so they honestly believed; they had struggled in vain against bad times; they had steadily come down in the world until, to put it bluntly, they had to take in lodgers. Dorothy had given her heart to a man whose name was never mentioned in the house, because he was looked upon as a "ne'er-do-weel." And now, to crown all, he had been caught in the toils of an absolutely hopeless love, and would have to nurse an unconfessed grief to the end of his days.

Ruby's soft, musical voice recalled him to himself again.

"It is not easy to thank people, is it?" she was saying. "But you will not think me ungrateful, will you? I can assure you I shall never forget that you saved my life."

"Please do not say any more, Miss Loveday," he interrupted. "I do not want to be thanked; I don't really. It will be the pleasantest memory of my life that I was able to render you a service."

"Then we understand each other," she said, with a smile. "And now we will talk about other things."

Justin by this time felt quite at his ease in Ruby's presence, and for a full hour conversation flowed freely and without a break. Ruby became more and more interested in him. She was surprised to discover how much he knew, and how well he could talk on matters that he was interested in. She had been inclined to think that only city people were clever and well informed, and that country-people were necessarily slow and altogether behind the age.

She had shed several illusions since she came into this western county, and some of her experiences had humbled her considerably. From henceforth she would think less and less of outside show. Polish was not everything, after all, especially when there was little or nothing underneath.

This Justin Pentyre, with his strong, grave face and his shy, hesitating manner, was not to be dismissed with a wave of the hand as though he were not worth a moment's thought. The longer she talked to him the more she became interested in him. He belonged to a type that she did not meet every day. His conversation was fresh and strong, like the wind that blew in from the Atlantic.

Moreover, he seemed to view many questions from what was to her an entirely new standpoint. She echoed the opinions of some London drawing-rooms, which she deemed almost infallible, and he laughingly shook his head and then proceeded very quietly and gently to turn them inside out.

So the minutes slipped away imperceptibly. She was so interested in having things set before her in a new light that she did not mind being worsted in argument.

"You will come and see me again, won't you?" she questioned, when at length he rose to take his leave.

"I will come as often as you will let me," he answered.

He knew he would be a moth scorching its wings every time he came into her presence, but

he could not help himself.   There was some
compensation in the pain, after all.

"I suppose you will be late home to-
morrow?" she questioned.

"I am afraid I shall be. Friday is our market-
day."

"And Saturday?"

"We keep open late on Saturday also."

"Then I must wait till Sunday."

"And I may come and see you on Sunday?"
he questioned, eagerly.

"I shall be very pleased if you will."

So they parted; and he walked through the
house into the orchard, his nerves tingling with
a new sensation, his heart throbbing with a new
joy, and yet a joy that was so near akin to pain
that he knew not whether to rejoice or be sorry.

CHAPTER X

A MERE NOBODY

"Jealousy is the forerunner of love,
And sometimes its awakener."

In a few days that which was merely "akin" to pain became a very acute agony. To love Ruby, even when there was not the smallest hope of winning her, was not without its compensations. He could dream about her all day long, and weave pretty fancies about her name ; he could pay her homage and win a smile from her now and then. He was not an intruder when he went to see her, for she had expressed a wish to see him.

But all this was quickly changed. On his return on the following evening Dorothy had news for him that affected him strangely.

"Who do you think has been here to-day?" she said, as he sat eating his supper.

"What a question, Dorothy," he answered, with a smile. "Half a score of people may have been here."

"Yes; but I was not thinking of St. Iago people. A stranger has been here from London?"

"To see me?"

"No; I don't think so. I fancy Ruby is the attraction."

"Oh, indeed. Any one that I know."

"Yes; you know him quite well."

"Do you mean Cousin Phil?"

"Yes."

For several minutes there was silence in the room. Justin appeared to be much more interested in his supper than he had been before. Dorothy watched him curiously for a moment, then took up a book she had been reading and began to turn its leaves.

Justin was the first to break the silence.

"Where's father?" he asked.

"He's gone to bed. You are so late home to-night."

"And mother?"

"She's somewhere about. You know mother is always busy whatever time of day it may be."

Another long silence followed. Then Justin spoke again.

"How is Phil looking?"

"Very well indeed. And what a handsome fellow he is! There is something in London, after all."

"Why do you say that?"

"Well, think of Phil's upbringing, and look at him now. Why, you would think he was 'to the manner born,' as they say. He is so easy, so self-possessed, so free from angularities. There is nothing shy or awkward about him. He seems to know always what is the right thing to do and the right thing to say."

"He has evidently impressed you to-day."

"Well, he has, Justin, in a way. The St. Iago young men, as a rule, never know what to do with their hands or feet, and will persist in standing when they ought to sit down, and when they do sit down always elect to make themselves uncomfortable on the extreme edge of the chair. Now, Phil was the opposite of all this. I was with Ruby when he was shown into the room, and I was struck with his grace of manner. He was frank, unobtrusive, sympathetic, and what he said to Ruby was in perfect taste."

"Indeed!"

"I am sure city life gives polish to a man."

"And evidently that is what women admire."

"Yes; no doubt they do, up to a certain point."

"And was Miss Loveday surprised to see him?"

"I don't think so. She seemed to take his coming as a matter of course. You know they

have known each other a very long time. It was
through Phil that the Lovedays came here."

"Yes; I know that. And you think she was
pleased to see him?"

"I am sure she was. You can always tell
when a girl is pleased. I have been wondering
ever since whether there is any kind of understanding between them. I feel sure Phil is very
fond of her."

"Likely enough. She is not a bad-looking
girl," he answered, without looking up from his
plate.

"Not bad-looking!" Dorothy said, reproachfully; "she is perfectly lovely, and the sweetest-
tempered creature I ever met."

To this he made no reply, and soon after took
himself off to bed. He was much more distressed by what he had heard than he yet realized.
The thought of Ruby being loved by another
and returning that love, struck deeper than he
knew. It is the surface wound that yields the
quickest pain. Wounds that are deep and
almost mortal are not felt at the moment.

He was tired and despondent, and even while
he was trying to probe the wound caused by
what he had heard he fell asleep.

The pain at his heart was much more acute
when he awoke next morning. He began to
understand what jealousy meant. He had read

about it in books, but as the day passed on he realized something of its torment; but it was not until the following day that the poison exercised all its strength.

He had looked forward to Sunday. Ruby had invited him to come to see her. The morning broke beautifully fine. The long summer seemed loath to depart. Justin awoke to the twittering of birds under the eaves and to the smell of ripe apples that floated in through his open window from the orchard.

The beautiful sunshine and the fresh, perfumed air were as a tonic to him. It was difficult to feel depressed on such a glorious morning. Perhaps he had been worrying himself over nothing. It was the most natural thing in the world that Phil, having business in Cornwall, should call at Endilloe. Perhaps Ruby cared nothing for him. Dorothy might be altogether mistaken.

He dressed himself in his very best. Perhaps by paying a little attention to details, he could look as well as Phil Passmore. He intended calling on Ruby soon after breakfast. Mr. Loveday was still in London, and Ruby might wish to be wheeled into the garden. She was still too lame to walk any distance.

He waited very impatiently for ten o'clock to strike. He learned from Dorothy that Ruby had got down to breakfast, and that she was looking wonderfully well, and was in excellent spirits.

He knocked very timidly at the Lovedays' door, and was at once admitted.

"I called to see if I could be of any service," he said, speaking rapidly. "I thought perhaps Miss Loveday would like to be wheeled into the garden—or—or—carried up into the orchard. It is lovely out-of-doors this morning," and he looked at Ruby, who was deep in an easy-chair, and tried not to feel embarrassed.

"It is very kind of you," Mrs. Loveday said, hesitatingly.

"Oh, it would be delightful," Ruby interrupted; "but it would be keeping you from chapel."

"Don't let that trouble you in the least," he answered quickly. "To tell you the truth, I am in no particular humour for chapel this morning."

"Then you can go to church if you like," Ruby said, turning to her mother. "I know you feel condemned unless you go once on the Sunday."

So it came to pass that Justin had Ruby all to himself, and so completely was he fascinated by her, that he forgot all about Phil Passmore, or if he thought about him at all, he supposed

H

that he was back again in London and quite out of the way.

After seeing Mrs. Loveday off the premises, he wheeled Ruby in her easy-chair out into the garden, and when the sun got too hot, he arranged a seat for her in the orchard and carried her thither in his arms.

For two hours and more he lived in Paradise, and resolutely bolted the door against the serpent and every other disturbing element. He knew only too well that his pleasure would soon come to an end, but he would not think of that now; he would make the most of it while it lasted.

Ruby looked her best, and was as gracious with him as he could desire. To be out in the sunshine once more was a real joy to her. No one could look into her face without realizing that she was supremely happy.

Justin waited upon her as though she had been a child. She expressed no wish that he did not try to gratify. He fetched flowers for her, and fruit, and books, and carried her anywhere and everywhere she desired to go; and when she wished to be still he sat at her feet, and read to her fragments from Hiawatha.

Now and then he glanced at her with eager, hungry eyes. She was so fair, so sweet, that

FOR TWO HOURS AND MORE HE LIVED IN PARADISE.

P. 112.

he felt he would give the world, did he possess it, even for the hope of winning her.

The moments sped away on feet of down, the hours passed like a dream; and with every passing moment the flame of his passion grew. He loved her before, but no word was strong enough to express what he felt now.

Ruby, all unconsciously, was binding him hand and foot. Had she known, she might have bestowed fewer smiles upon him, and asked for less attention. But she was only a girl in her own eyes, and this strong, sober-eyed young man seemed almost old to her, and she never imagined for a moment that he would ever think of love.

So she allowed him to pay her all the attention he desired to pay, and she accepted it with gratitude and without misgiving. It was very pleasant to be waited on; to be carried in his big, strong arms; to have all her wishes carried out; to have even the glance of her eye interpreted aright.

She grew more and more interested in him as the morning wore away. He was no common man. He did not reveal himself in a moment. There were depths that a mere stranger would not suspect. Every now and then his grave eyes would light up with a hidden and unsuspected fire.

Nevertheless he kept himself well in hand; it was his business to do that. This sweet-eyed girl must never know the truth.

He carried her back into the garden in time for her to greet her mother on her return from church, and, a little later, wheeled her back into the house.

Early in the afternoon he presented himself before Ruby again, and was suggesting that they should repeat the experience of the morning, when a visitor was announced, and the next moment, bland, handsome, and smiling, Phil Passmore came into the room. He greeted Justin with effusion, and Ruby and her mother with every manifestation of pleasure; and then, without being obtrusive, he seemed to monopolize everything. Justin felt as though a bucket of cold water had been thrown over him. The whole atmosphere of the place seemed to change in a minute, and he changed along with it. The presence of Phil froze every current of thought and speech; he felt awkward, and diffident, and out of place.

Not so, however, with the others. Mrs. Loveday seemed delighted to see her guest again. She was utterly tired of being cooped up in a farmhouse, and was pining for her London home and the life and movement of the big city.

"I did not know you were staying so long in Cornwall," she said.

"I did not know myself when I came," he answered, with a gay laugh. But one must be prepared for delays when he gets down into this slow-moving place."

"And will you be returning soon?" Ruby questioned.

"To-morrow, or Tuesday at the latest. But let me congratulate you on your improved appearance. You are looking a lot better than you did on Thursday. You are, really."

"I am getting better every day. I hope to get home next week."

"It will be a treat to see you in London again," he said, warmly. "You don't know how we have missed you."

"I shall be glad to see all the old faces again," she said, with a smile. "It has been very trying, shut up in one little room for so long."

"I wonder you have not pined yourself to death," he answered, with a laugh. "But we shall see you in the Park again before the summer is ended."

Then the conversation drifted away to matters that Justin knew nothing about. They discussed places and people with great animation and gaiety; they referred to events he had never heard of before. He felt himself outside the charmed circle; he was an interloper and an intruder.

He edged himself nearer and nearer the door, and no one seemed to notice his movement. Conversation was flowing freely and embroidered with little ripples of laughter. Whether he went or stayed was a matter of no moment to anybody. He was a mere nonentity. Ruby had forgotten him, to all appearance—forgotten the errand on which he had come.

He grew hot and cold by turns, for he had all the Pentyre's family pride, and was acutely sensitive. He mentally contrasted his appearance with that of his cousin Phil. His best clothes, which were now two summers old, were positively shabby by the side of Phil's well-fitting suit; neither had he the easy grace of manner and conversation that his cousin had. How gliby he talked. How familiar he was with the Lovedays, and yet not too familiar. How absolutely he monopolized the conversation, and yet never seemed obtrusive.

Yes; all that Dorothy had said was quite true. The city man had the advantage. He was good enough to entertain Ruby while there was no one better near, but directly Phil appeared upon the scene he was forgotten.

He clenched his fists till the nails made

marks in the palms of his hands. He tried to hate the Lovedays, and his cousin, and every one connected with them. And yet all the while Ruby's low, musical voice stirred his heart with a strange rapture and filled him with an inexpressible longing.

What a contrast between the afternoon and the morning! Then he was in Paradise, now he was in Purgatory. Then love alone dominated him and filled the world with sunshine. Now jealousy—mad, unreasoning jealousy—tore him like a legion of devils.

He was now close to the door, which stood ajar. No one noticed him or addressed a single question to him. Ruby's face was towards him —a bright, animated face; but her eyes were fixed on Phil. Mrs. Loveday was looking at her visitor from another angle of the room, while Phil himself, handsome, confident, was for the moment monarch of all he surveyed.

Justin could bear it no longer. He felt crushed, humiliated, and stung almost to madness. He stepped back and back, till the door stood between him and the others. Then he paused and listened. But the conversation flowed on without a break, and the snatches of laughter rang out as before. He was a nobody.

He walked straight through the house into the orchard, and from thence across the field up into the plantation; but he was too restless, too angry to remain still anywhere. In a few minutes he was out on the cliff, pacing restlessly up and down. Then he descended to the beach, and walked out on the sand until the green curling waves stopped his further progress.

Why was it that Phil Passmore was preferred before himself? Phil had not saved Ruby. Phil had not risked his life on her behalf, and he was sure that he did not love her as he did. Oh, it was intolerable to be slighted and thrust aside just because he was poor and could not dress in the latest fashion.

But why was he poor? Of course he would always be poor if he remained in a sleepy little village like Trelford. There was no scope for a man where he was. Phil would have been no better off than he if he had remained at home.

He sat down on a rock at length, and tried to think calmly and dispassionately. He did not heed the sinking sun or the voice of the incoming tide. Slowly a desperate resolution was taking shape in his brain, which was destined to have further-reaching consequences than either he or any one else could see.

CHAPTER XI

A NEW DEPARTURE

> " I am very content with knowing,
> If only I could know."

Autumn deepened into winter and Christmas came without anything happening to disturb the quiet of Endilloe. The Lovedays returned to London before the chill of autumn began to be felt, and now and then Ruby wrote to Dorothy and gave her sundry particulars about the life she was leading and the prospects of the season, which promised to be more than usually gay.

Justin went on with his work as though nothing had happened. To a close observer he seemed a little quieter than usual. But no one guessed how deeply he had been smitten by Ruby's beauty, or how constantly he pined for a sight of her face. He said nothing to any one of the plans and schemes which agitated his brain and kept him awake at nights. But the purpose that shaped itself in his mind that memorable

Sunday evening down by the sea he never relinquished. Day and night he brooded over it, and waited impatiently for his chance to come.

Dorothy, having no visitors to wait upon, spent more time than usual in thinking of her truant lover, the "ne'er-do-weel" of the parish, the bright, happy, lazy, generous scamp, whom everybody loved and blamed at the same time, and whose utter ruin was regarded as a foregone conclusion.

He had left her, not exactly in anger, though strong words had passed between them.

"You are like the rest of them, Dorothy," he said; "you have no faith in me;" and his face flushed and his lips trembled as he spoke. "Perhaps you are right. Heaven only knows. Anyhow, neither you nor any one else shall ever see me in St. Iago again until I have proved whether I am worth anything or no;" and he strode off into the darkness.

Dorothy called after him, but he did not heed. That was a year and a half ago, and no one had either seen or heard of Tom Pendarvis since.

His name was never mentioned at Endilloe, for John Pentyre had forbidden him the house before that night when he so abruptly bade Dorothy good-bye.

Yet Dorothy never wavered in her love and

loyalty to him. She was not like the rest; she had faith in him. He might be gay, and reckless, and improvident, and idle; she did not deny any of the charges. But she believed there was latent goodness in him, too—latent energy and strength and endurance. She half-wondered sometimes—when everybody spoke ill of him—whether the goodness was only in the eyes of the beholder; whether love saw what it sought for and discovered what had no real existence. But her doubts were never more than for a moment. She could always find an excuse for him. He had been unfortunate; had been left an orphan when he most needed a guiding hand, and when he was only half though his apprenticeship as an engineer. Had Dr. Pendarvis lived, everything would have been different. But Tom would come out right in the end; she had no doubt of that.

So she cherished his memory in silence; and waited with as much patience as she could command.

Now and then she and Justin talked of the Lovedays, but she never guessed that he had lost his heart to Ruby.

"I don't expect they will ever come to Endilloe again," he said one day, with apparent indifference.

"Very likely not," she answered. "And yet

I do not think we shall ever quite lose sight of them."

"Why so?"

"Well, I feel sure Cousin Phil intends to win Ruby, and I think he will succeed in the long run."

"In the long run?" he questioned. "Do you think he will have any difficulty at the start."

"Well, I don't know, Justin," she said, with a laugh. "I thought at first there was some kind of understanding between them, but I am sure now that I was mistaken. She is little more than a girl, after all, and won't know her own mind yet. But anybody can see that Phil is very fond of her, so what's to hinder a match in the long run?"

"Some other fellow may come along more to her mind," he answered, carelessly.

"That's possible, of course. But he appears to have the run of the house, and that counts for a good deal."

"How wisely you talk," he said, with a laugh; and then the subject dropped.

But he did not forget what she said, and it influenced him more than he knew. Constantly, and at the most unexpected times, the question would leap to his lips, "Why may I not win her?" and the answer would come sharp as a flash. In fact, there were a dozen answers to his unspoken hope, all of them sound and logical and almost irresistible. When he reasoned he fell into despair, for Ruby seemed as much out of his reach as the North Pole. But hope does not depend upon reason, and so he went on dreaming day after day, and building his castles in the air, and making plans that, to the prudent and worldly-wise, would appear idiotic.

It was not until after Christmas that his resolve began to take definite shape. He had made any number of applications, and answered scores of advertisements, but at last his chance had come.

When he announced to the little family circle that he was leaving home on New Year's Day to take up a situation in London, they were struck dumb. It was the last thing in the world they ever expected to hear. Dorothy protested that he was joking as soon as she had recovered herself; but Mrs. Pentyre walked out of the room to indulge in the luxury of a cry, for she knew that when Justin said a thing he meant it, and it seemed to her the beginning of the end. It was the first break in the family, the first bird to fly away from the old nest. Life at Endilloe would never be the same again.

John Pentyre looked on and said nothing.

He was a quiet man at best. Moreover, he had great faith in Justin, and believed that he would not take such an important step without very sufficient reasons. Nevertheless, John troubled most of all when Justin went away. He saw the end of the Pentyres' reign at Endilloe. It is true he had never encouraged Justin to be a farmer, for the ground-landlord wrung the last penny out of his tenants, and made life for them all but intolerable. Yet, for all that, it was a bitter pain to him to see the long succession broken. For generations the Pentyres had occupied Endilloe, and once upon a time had owned the land for many a rich acre in all directions, though now only the house was left to them, with the garden and orchard, and one or two small meadows. Yet the memory of past greatness still remained, and it was galling to the pride to see the chain snapped short and to know that after his day the names "Endilloe" and "Pentyre" would no longer be associated.

He said nothing to Justin of what he felt as he drove him to the station. It was of no use bemoaning what could not be helped. He had seen it coming since the day Justin had decided that he would not be a farmer. Only now it was accentuated and brought into bold and painful relief. The tears were very near his eyes on the outward drive, and some of them fell silently and unobserved as he drove home alone.

Justin told no one the whole of his reasons for going away; he had hardly the courage to confess them to himself. But lying down at the bottom of all was his love for Ruby and his desire to be near her. He knew absolutely nothing about London, but he had a vague idea that he would be able now and then to get within seeing distance of the girl he loved, and feast his eyes once and awhile upon her beauty.

But beyond all that was another hope. He might win a position in London. Other people had done so, why might not he? Phil Passmore had absolutely nothing when he journeyed up to London. Now he was a gentleman, able to visit Ruby as an equal. And was it altogether unreasonable to argue that what had been done might be done again? He owned that the time was short, that unless he made a position for himself in a year or two Ruby would have passed for ever out of his reach. He admitted, also, that worshipping Ruby at a distance was scarcely an effective method of winning her.

Indeed, the whole situation would not bear looking at in the cold light of reason. The chances were a thousand to one against the success of his enterprise. It was on that one odd chance that he built his hopes. If that failed him there remained an open door and a welcome at Endilloe.

It was a tedious journey to London, for the weather was bitterly cold, with a keen north wind that found its way through every crack and cranny of the railway carriage. He was sad of heart, too, for the wrench of leaving home was greater than he had anticipated. He never knew how much he loved the old place until he had to say good-bye; and when the final parting came he half regretted the decision he had come to. It was too late, however, to draw back. He had made his choice and would have to abide by it. It was a relief, however, when the train began to move out of the station, and he saw his father's sad, pathetic face fading in the distance. He waved his hand as the train was sweeping round the curve, then he closed the window and sat back in his corner and closed his eyes.

It grew dark long before the train reached Bristol, and the rest of the journey seemed a reckless plunging into the darkness. He had never travelled in an express before, and the speed made him nervous. He would not have minded had it been daylight, but this wild swirl and leap in the night seemed to set his nerves on edge. But it came to an end at last.

First of all, the stations got thicker on the ground, then long lines of gas-lamps stretched away in the distance. Then his fellow-passengers began to get their belongings together. Cloth caps were exchanged for tall hats, and bags and bundles were lifted from the racks and placed on the seats.

Justin's heart was in a strange tumult. This great London that he had so often heard of and read about began to affect him strangely. It was all a plunge into the darkness. He was half afraid. The place was full of sharpers, he had been told, who were always waiting to pounce on young people from the country.

He kept his hand on his portmanteau. It contained all his belongings. Now the train began to slow up, and the myriad lights of the great city were twinkling in all directions. At last. And, oh, what a hubbub! He stood for several seconds with his portmanteau in his hand, not knowing which way to turn. He refused the help of a porter; he was afraid to trust any one in this strange place. Nobody, however, heeded him much; every one was intent on his own affairs. He could hardly help envying the people who seemed just as much at home as he would feel in Trelford. Gentlemen and ladies too jumped into hansoms and were off like a shot, while he stood there with his heart in his mouth and wondered if he would ever find his way to Cheapside.

He could not help thinking of Amos Blue's last words to him.

"I hope, Maister Justin," he had said, "that when you do get up to London Station you will look out for our Dan'l."

"But London is a very big place, Amos," he had replied.

"Iss, iss; so they do tell me. But our Dan'l is very good to knaw. His 'air is terrible red, an' he's muffly all over his face."

"Yes, I know," Justin remarked.

"An' you tell 'im for we, that is, for me an' his mother, that it is quite time he wrot' to us. We be quite pinin' for a letter from 'im."

"I will tell him if I see him, Amos."

"Oh, but you be sure to see him, Maister Justin, an' he is good to knaw is our Dan'l. An' spaik strong to 'im 'bout honouring his father and mother."

A momentary smile flitted across Justin's face at the remembrance of Amos's message, but he quickly grew grave again. He had never felt so lost, forsaken, alone, in his life before. On every side people were hurrying, rushing, jostling, intent on getting to their destination by the most expeditious method, while he stood still bewildered, yet fascinated by the scene.

At length he espied a policeman, and made for him. The policeman was civil even to kindness. He pointed the way to Praed Street Station, and even went some distance with him.

While he was fumbling for change to pay for his ticket, he saw a train come in and go out again, and for the moment he thought he was stranded for the night; but he soon learnt otherwise.

He nearly missed the next train while he rushed up and down the platform for some official who would tell him if it stopped at Aldersgate Street. At last, however, he was on the move again, plunging into smoke and sulphur, squealing, shrieking, out into the open for a few moments, then burrowing underground again. He wondered where he was being taken to. The journey seemed interminable. At length he ventured to inquire of a fellow-passenger.

"Next station but one," was the quick reply. "This is King's Cross;" and the man jumped out of the train, bolted across the platform, and into another train, which was just moving out in the opposite direction.

"These people seem to know their way about," he reflected. "I wonder if I shall ever get used to it."

At Aldersgate Street a porter hunted up a

hansom for him, and at length, after what to him was an intensely exciting ride, he found himself at his destination. Here one of the assistants took him in hand, and showed him his cubicle at the top of the house, and then brought him down to a big dining-room and set him before a joint of cold meat, which he was allowed to carve for himself.

Man though he was, he had great difficulty in keeping back the tears when he got into bed. The sweet privacy of his own little room at Endilloe was at an end. Why had he left it for this great wilderness of a city? Even his love for Ruby was not sufficient at the moment to keep back a great surging wave of regret that swept over him.

CHAPTER XII

A GLIMPSE OF PARADISE

> " I know not how others saw her,
> But to me she was always fair."

JUSTIN's letters home were eagerly read by the little family circle, and freely discussed; but opinion was divided as to whether he was pleased or disappointed, hopeful or despondent. They contained any number of generalities about the big city, and the big house of business in which he was one of legion, but very little that was definite about himself.

Mrs. Pentyre searched eagerly for some note of disappointment. She wanted her boy home again; and every day she kept hoping that he would tire of the noise and crowd and find his way back to Endilloe again, a sadder and a wiser man. But if Justin felt any disappointment he kept it to himself. He assured them constantly that he was gaining experience, that he was getting enlarged views of business methods and operations, that he was extending his knowledge of men and things; but he did not say that he had found in London all he had expected, and that he was glad he had come.

As a matter-of-fact, that was a question he had not yet settled in his own mind. There was a good deal to be said on both sides. He never pretended to himself that he was happy or content. Sometimes, indeed, he felt very miserable. But the present was not everything; it was of the future he thought most. The long hours and uncongenial surroundings were but a means to an end, though it was in no way clear how such means could lead to the end he had in view. He had come to London to make his fortune, and win Ruby Loveday. But whoever made a fortune serving as an assistant behind a counter? He was but one of a hundred others in the same establishment, and, for all he knew, they were all of them inspired by similar hopes. Many of them, like himself, had come up from the country. Doubtless they all had their dreams of success; they were all possible Dick Whittingtons. They pictured prosperity and unbounded wealth in the future. On how many of them would Fortune smile?

He always grew despondent when he looked at the matter in the cold light of reason. His hope lay in the unexpected. Fortune was rarely

reached along the humdrum path of toil. Something might turn up at the most unlikely time.
His business was to do his best, and hold on
to his hope.

So the dull days dragged painfully away.
He worked hard, tried to look cheerful, and did
his best to give satisfaction to his employers;
but whether he succeeded or not in this particular he was by no means certain. It was
not altogether easy to fall into Cheapside ways.
He had been used to something so totally different, and, in his own judgment, to something
very much better; and some of the London
methods he had no wish to learn.

But during all those dull days he saw no
road to fortune, and in Cheapside he felt as
far away from Ruby almost as he did in
Cornwall. He had no time to go anywhere or
see anything. When closing-time came it was
too late and too dark to set out on a voyage
of exploration, and during the first five or six
weeks every Saturday afternoon had been
miserable with rain and snow.

How much he pined for the country during
those miserable days of January and February
he never confessed, even to himself. Most
evenings he went out for a walk—generally
alone—but there was no pleasure in it. The
miles and miles of twinkling lights that stretched

away in every direction oppressed him. He was afraid to go too far away, lest he should not be able to find his way back again ; so for several weeks he got no farther than London Bridge in one direction and Ludgate Circus in the other. Then gradually he extended his journeys. He got to Temple Bar, and then to Trafalgar Square, and then to Piccadily Circus. The life of London, particularly in the evenings, lay westward. The city itself was almost deserted. On Sundays he kept up his old habit and went regularly to church or chapel, and he had not to go far, and generally there was no lack of accommodation ; but he missed the warmth, and fervour, and homeliness of the little Methodist chapel at St. Iago.

His attempts to get an interview with his cousin proved a failure. Phil's city address was 92, Melton Friars. He was several weeks in finding the narrow court in the heart of the city, and when he did find it all the offices were closed. On Saturday afternoons the city emptied itself early, consequently Justin was always too late. He was somewhat disconcerted also to find that No. 92 was occupied by Mead, Runcorn, Jago and Co.

He read the names on the door-plates several times over, and then asked himself where Phil Passmore came in. There was nothing in the style of the firm to suggest his cousin, except the name Jago, which was the usual corruption of Iago. What could it mean? Was Phil merely a subordinate, or was he trading under an assumed name? He felt considerably perplexed and not a little troubled. What business the firm carried on there was nothing to indicate.

He made up his mind not to write to his cousin. He wanted to come upon him unawares and see his look of surprise.

But while he was anxious to see Phil, he was still more anxious to see Ruby. He had asked Dorothy not to mention the fact in her letters that he was in London; he intended also paying the Lovedays a surprise visit at some favourable opportunity. Had he consulted his inclinations, he would have hunted them up the first Saturday he was in London. But he concluded that it would be much more seemly if he waited awhile. He was anxious not to convey the impression that he wanted something, or that he was presuming upon a mere chance acquaintanceship.

It is true that all the Lovedays had said to him again and again that if he ever came to London he must be sure and call upon them. But how much that meant he did not know. City nabobs, as a rule, were not anxious to entertain their country cousins; and he was not at all sure that the Lovedays would be pleased to see him.

Nevertheless, he resolved to call when he had familiarized himself a little with London ways. How else would he ever see Ruby; and if he never saw her, what was the use of coming to London at all? By the end of Feburary he was beginning to feel at home in London streets. The crowds no longer oppressed him, and the noise had ceased to jar upon his nerves. The last Saturday in February proved to be beautifully fine, and Justin attired himself in his latest London-made suit, and directly business closed made his way towards Regent's Park.

It was an unknown part of London to him, and it gave him a new idea of its magnitude and wealth. St. Winifred's Terrace commanded a view of the Park, so that he had no difficulty in finding it, though he was far longer in reaching it than he had ever anticipated. He had no idea that the Park was so vast. In walking across it, he felt for the moment that he was out in the country again, miles away from the noise and grime of the city.

No. 10 was like every other house in the terrace, stuccoed and painted drab. It stood back a few feet from the pavement, allowing room for an area, and a flight of steps to the door, which was shaded by a heavy porch.

Justin felt his heart beating very fast as he approached the house. For five long months he had been pining for a sight of Ruby's face. Now, perhaps, his hope would be realized. It was possible that in a few minutes more he would be standing in her presence, feasting his eyes upon her beauty and thrilling at the music of her voice.

He ran up the steps with a show of confidence that he did not by any means feel, and gave the bell-handle a vigorous pull. In a few minutes the door was opened by a maid-servant daintily dressed.

"No; Mr. and Mrs. Loveday were out."

Justin's heart felt like a lump of lead.

"Was Miss Loveday at home?"

"She was, but——"

"Perhaps she will see me," he interrupted. "Will you take her my card?"

The girl hesitated for a moment, then turned and walked up the broad stairs, and left Justin standing at the door. His heart was still beating uncomfortably fast, and an uneasy feeling took possession of him that he might be regarded as an unwelcome visitor.

He was not left long in doubt, however. In a few moments a light step sounded on the stairs, and, looking up, he saw Ruby herself coming towards him, radiant and smiling.

"Why, this is an unexpected pleasure, Mr. Pentyre," she said, extending both her hands to him. "Who ever expected to see you in London? And how is Dorothy? And how did you come? But come up into the drawing-room. Father and mother are making a call this afternoon, but they will be back for dinner."

So she chatted as she led the way up the broad stairs, while Justin followed like one in a dream. Ruby's beauty seemed more dazzling than ever, and her welcome was warmer than he had ever expected in his most optimistic moments.

The drawing-room was large and handsomely furnished. A big fire was burning at the farther end, and Ruby wheeled up an easy-chair in front of it.

"I am sure you must be cold," she said. "I will order afternoon tea at once. How fortunate that I am at home. I should have gone out with the others, but I have been at the ambulance class all the morning, and felt rather tired."

Justin dropped mechanically into the chair, and wondered if he were quite wideawake.

Ruby rang the bell and ordered tea to be brought, then she drew up a chair opposite him and looked at him. She was as ingenuous as a

child, and, fortunately for her, she had no suspicion of Justin's love. In her heart she was
genuinely glad to see him again. He would
always be more or less of a hero in her eyes.
She could not forget how he had let himself
down by a rope to the bottom of a deep shaft in
search of her, and how, later, he had found her,
bruised and helpless, almost surrounded by the
sea. In the months that had since passed, her
imagination had often been busy, and she had
realized her peril far more vividly than she did
at the first.

Justin looked at her, and the fire of his love
flamed into a white heat. He felt as though he
would give everything—even his hope of heaven
—for the chance of calling her his.

"And now tell me all about Endilloe," Ruby
said, locking her hands across her knee. "When
did you come up?"

"I came on the first of January," he said.

".The first of January?" she questioned.
"Why, that is nearly two months ago."

"Yes. Time creeps along slowly."

"Then you are living in London?"

"Yes; like many another man, I have come
up to seek my fortune."

She turned away her eyes from him and
looked into the fire, and for a few moments there
was silence between them.

"Do you think it is worth while?" she asked at length, without looking at him.

He did not quite understand her, and so he began to talk about the lack of opportunity that such a place as Trelford offered, and the impossibility of bettering his position in such a small and out-of-the-way place.

"And what do you hope to do in London?" she questioned, raising her clear, earnest eyes to his.

"Ah," he said, colouring slightly. "If I were to tell you of all my hopes and dreams you would laugh at me."

"But you would like to get rich like the rest of them?"

"Yes," he answered, candidly, "I should."

For a moment she was silent, and again looked from him into the fire.

"Does it ever strike you as strange," she said at length, "that all the world should be running after money?"

"But we cannot do without it," he said, uneasily.

"But do we need so much? Were you not happy at home?"

"Ah, that raises a very big question," he answered. "In many ways, I was very happy at home. I sometimes wonder if I shall ever be so happy again. And if I could have—have

—forgotten—that—is—if—if—I had no desire—beyond—beyond—well, St. Iago, shall I say? —I might have been content to have remained at home always."

She noticed that he was getting confused, that he was blushing painfully, so she turned her attention to the fire, and began to poke it with considerable vigour.

"I hope you will not think I am a mere money-grubber," he said, hurriedly. "I don't think I am that. It is not the money itself that I care for, but it might—I don't know, of course, but it might—help me to realize what I do care for very much. When a man is poor, there are things he dare not hope for."

"But are those things the best things?" she asked.

"I think so," he answered, slowly. "I may be mistaken, of course, but it seems to me that I am right."

"Perhaps you are," she said, after a long pause. "And yet, do you know, since I have been back here in London again, I have almost envied you the quiet, peaceful life you led at Endilloe. Here every one seems so eager, so restless, so dissatisfied. Oh, I know we live in big houses, and all that. But money is not everything, I am sure."

"No, not everything; but if you knew what

poverty was, pitiless, grinding, demoralizing poverty, you would not wonder that people dread it and seek to rise above it."

"Oh, extremes are bad in everything," she said, looking up with a smile. "But here comes the tea. Now we shall be able to gossip to our hearts' content."

Justin looked at her admiringly, but did not reply. How dainty she was, how sweet and wholesome and unspoilt! Moreover, she had revealed herself in a new light this afternoon. She was evidently not a mere society butterfly, thinking only of dress and fashion and pleasure. In her own way she had evidently been trying to get below the surface of things.

"I should dearly like to go down into Cornwall again next summer," she said, handing him a cup of tea. "But I'm afraid it's out of the question. "Father wants us to go to Norway."

"I was afraid you would never want to go to Cornwall again," he said; "you seemed so eager to get away from it."

"Of course, I was anxious to get home; and yet I have not enjoyed the season as I expected I should. It has been gay enough. But a lot of things we call pleasure are really nothing of the kind. We go the rounds because it is the proper thing. We are the slaves of custom;" and she sat down opposite him and began to sip her tea.

Poor Justin hovered between Paradise and the Inferno. He loved her more than ever, and yet in this beautiful house, with its rich appointments, she seemed doubly and trebly out of his reach.

Then a knock came to the door, and a moment later Mr. Phil Passmore was announced.

K

CHAPTER XIII

AN UNEXPECTED MEETING

"Alas for him who flings away
  The shield of purity."

AT the mention of Phil's name Justin grew cold all over. He was the one man at the moment he did not want to see. His presence would be like a false note in music. The sweet harmony of the afternoon would be at an end.

Phil came bland and smiling into the room, but on catching sight of Justin his face suddenly clouded and his eyes looked unutterable things. It was but for a moment, however. The cloud passed as suddenly as it came, though Justin felt that his greeting was far less cordial than it was wont to be.

Ruby received her guest with a certain shyness and reserve that Justin was quick to notice, but did not know how to interpret. Was it the natural shyness of a maiden welcoming her lover, or——

But he had no time to debate the question

then. Phil was not shy; in fact, he appeared to be quite at home—too much at home for Justin's peace of mind. He received his cup of tea as a matter of course, and then turned his attention to Justin.

"You did not let me know you were coming up?" he said, in a questioning tone.

"No; I had no opportunity."

"Of course, you are not staying long?"

There was something in the manner in which this was said that struck Justin unpleasantly and sent him back into his shell.

"A few days longer," he answered, evasively and shortly.

"You should have let me know you were coming," Phil said, suavely, "and I would have made arrangements for showing you the sights of London."

"Unfortunately, I have very little time for sightseeing," was the answer. "Besides, I did not wish to make myself a burden to anybody."

"Tut! tut! You should not talk about being a burden. Am I not your first cousin?"

"But that gives me no right to encroach upon your time, though I should like to call upon you if you have an evening to spare."

"Ah, just so. A very good idea. Let me think. Unfortunately, every evening next week is taken up. You should have let me know beforehand that you were coming up, then we could have arranged it. But I'll see about it. Shall I trouble you for another cup of tea?" turning to Ruby. "Thank you very much. I don't know when I have tasted anything so refreshing."

Five minutes later Justin felt, as on a former occasion, that he was out in the cold. Phil monopolized the conversation and Ruby also. The talk drifted away to subjects that he knew nothing about. Ruby appeared to become so interested that she did not notice that Justin sat dumb. Phil kept the ball rolling with amazing dexterity, now and then addressing himself to Justin but giving him no chance of reply.

The position became intolerable at length, and he rose abruptly from his seat.

"You are surely not going yet?" Ruby said, rising also. "Father and mother will be back——"

Then the louder voice of Phil chimed in— "Sorry you have to go, Justin, but I know what it means when a fellow is up on business——"

"But I took it for granted that you would stay to dinner," Ruby interposed. "You surely——"

"You'll remember me to all at home, Justin, if I should not see you again," broke in the louder voice of Phil. "I'm awfully sorry you've dropped on me at such a busy time."

And somehow the louder voice prevailed, as it often does in this world. Those who can shout the loudest often get most attention.

While Ruby was thinking what she should say next, Phil went and opened the door.

It was a hurried and clumsy leave-taking. Justin managed to say to Ruby that he would call again, and then, without quite knowing how, he found himself descending the stairs, and a minute later the street door closed behind him.

For some distance he walked on, not knowing where he was, or caring. The twin demons of jealousy and despair seemed to be tearing him to pieces.

"Oh, I've no chance!" he muttered to himself, bitterly. "She's kind and gracious, and all that; but that's her nature. Oh, I wish I'd never seen her, then I might have been content to jog along in the old ruts to the end of the journey! Now I'm trying to catch a comet;" and he clenched his hands savagely.

A few minutes later, he contradicted himself flatly.

"I'm glad I've seen her," he said, raising his head and smiling. "And isn't she lovely? Life is worth the living, if only for the chance of looking at her now and then, and seeing her smile."

So he alternated between hope and despair,

between Paradise and Purgatory. There were times when he believed that she cared for him as much as she cared for Phil—perhaps more; for had he not saved her life? And she would not be likely to forget that. At other times he was fully persuaded that Phil was her accepted lover, and that he had no right to bestow another thought upon her.

On that point, however, he resolved to satisfy himself at the earliest opportunity. By some means or other he must find out if any understanding existed between them.

During that night he scarcely slept at all. Try as he would, he could not help thinking that he had come to London on a fool's errand. His conduct always looked worse in the darkness than it did in the daylight. Supposing Phil had not to be reckoned with. Supposing Ruby, instead of favouring him, hated him—what then? Even if Phil were out of the way, his chance would scarcely be improved. He had seen her in her home; and how could he ever hope to make a home for her like that? He was earning barely enough to maintain himself, and he saw no chance of improving his position for many years to come, if ever. Meanwhile, the very idea of a shop-assistant aspiring to the hand of a merchant's daughter seemed too ridiculous to be regarded seriously.

Nevertheless—such inconsistent creatures are we all—next morning being Sunday, and fine, he started off again for Regent's Park. It was not difficult to keep an eye on the Lovedays' house without being noticed. He wanted to find out what church they attended, and whether Phil attended the same place of worship, and whether he joined the family circle after service, and went home with them to lunch.

A few minutes before eleven he saw Mr. and Mrs. Loveday and Ruby descend the steps and walk slowly up the street. To follow them without being noticed was not difficult. In a few minutes they had entered a church, and were lost to sight.

"That is a point gained," he reflected. "But if I am seen here by Phil he will accuse me of all sorts of things;" and he walked rapidly away till he came to another church, which he entered.

The service proved to be short, and he was back again in time to see the Lovedays come out. He gave a little sigh of relief when he discovered that Phil was not with them; and then hurried off to Portland Road Station, and got home in time for dinner.

He did not go to Regent's Park again for two or three weeks. He felt a little bit ashamed of himself; yet all the while he was pining for a sight of Ruby's face. Towards the middle of March he got a half-day off, and he was not two seconds in making up his mind what to do with it.

There was already a touch of spring in the air as he walked across the Park, and a grateful, earthy smell from the newly turned flower-beds. It made him think of Endilloe, and stirred his heart with a painful longing to see the old place again. It was only for a moment, however. He was going to see Ruby; and that thought banished everything else from his mind.

"Being Wednesday," he reflected, "I am not likely to be thwarted by Phil Passmore, unless he calls every day in the week, which is not at all probable."

He slackened his pace when the terrace came into sight through the leafless trees. He was wondering if the Lovedays would be at home, and whether they would think he was presuming upon a chance acquaintance in calling a second time.

"I know I am not of their set," he reflected; "but Ruby asked me to call, and I promised her I would; but I shall soon discover if I am not wanted;" and he walked on still more slowly, with his eyes bent upon the ground.

Suddenly he looked up with a start and an

exclamation of surprise. Standing before him
was Ruby, her lips parted in one of her most
gracious smiles.

"Well, this is an unexpected pleasure!" she
said. "Who would have thought of seeing you
out here?"

"I had a few hours off from business to-day,"
he said, blushing; "and one seems to get a sniff
of the country here."

"And the smell of spring is already in the
air," she replied. "Oh, I am always glad when
the spring comes."

"You are fortunate in living so near the
Park," he said.

"You think so?"

"There can be no doubt of it. Cheapside
makes one hunger for a glimpse of green grass
and the sight of a tree, though I believe there
is one tree not far away from us. I have not
noticed it myself, but, at any rate, there is a
tradition to that effect."

She gave a little laugh, then abruptly turned
the conversation.

"You were going to call on us, of course.
We have all been wondering when your promised
visit was to be paid. Father would have written
you, but you left no address."

"I should like to call very much, but I see
you are going out."

"Only into Marylebone Road. I shall be back again in half an hour."

"May I walk with you?" he said, wondering at his temerity.

"If you don't mind," she answered, brightly; "but, as a rule, gentlemen don't like waiting outside shops."

"I don't mind in the least," he said; and they walked away together.

They were much more than half an hour in going and returning, but to Justin it did not seem five minutes. He wished the streets would lengthen out indefinitely. To walk by the side of this sweet-faced maiden, as though he were her equal, was like a dream to him, and again came the old question: "Could he win her? Could he make himself worthy of her? Could he hope that fortune might smile upon him, and work a wonder on his behalf?"

Then his thoughts flew off to Phil. Did he stand in his way? How could he get to know?

"Have you seen your cousin lately?" The question came suddenly and unexpectedly.

"Not since I saw him at your house," he answered, colouring slightly.

"Then you have not told him that you are living in London?"

"No; I have really had no chance."

"But why did you evade it when you were at our house?"

"I don't know," he answered, frankly. "It was his manner, I think. He irritated me somewhat."

"I thought you did not seem quite yourself."

For a few moments there was silence, then he said, abruptly—

"Have you seen him lately?"

"Oh yes;" and she laughed a merry little laugh. "He drops in once or twice every week —sometimes oftener."

"Lucky dog, Phil!" The next moment she had rung the door-bell.

"I found Mr. Pentyre walking unprotected in the Park," she said to her mother, with a gay laugh, "so I took compassion on him and brought him home."

Nothing could have been kinder than Mrs. Loveday's welcome, and Justin found himself once more peeping through the gates of Paradise. An hour later Mr. Loveday returned. Justin thought he looked worried and anxious; and for awhile he talked about certain international complications that were upsetting business and causing commercial men no end of anxiety. But over the dinner-table the talk drifted back to Cornwall, and foreign complications and business anxieties appeared to be forgotten. Justin not only peeped through the gates, but he seemed to get inside. After dinner Ruby played and sang, and the evening sped away like a dream. And when he left, Mr. Loveday gave him a very pressing invitation to come again.

Instead of taking the Underground, he got into a 'bus and dreamt away the journey to Trafalgar Square. Now and then he roused himself and called himself a fool, but he quickly went back to his dreams again.

It was getting late when he got to Trafalgar Square, but he decided, nevertheless, that he would walk the rest of the way. The Strand was comparatively empty, for most of the theatres had closed.

He walked along at a rapid pace, then paused suddenly.

" I know that voice," he said to himself.

A well-dressed man was reeling on in front of him, with a woman holding fast to his arm.

He hurried on again, and came close to the couple. The voice was Phil Passmore's—there could be no doubt of that. Thick and guttural it might be, but unmistakably his.

But to make doubly sure, he crossed the street and walked rapidly ahead, then re-crossed it and met the pair where the light of a lamp fell full upon their faces.

There was no longer any room for doubt now. Phil was evidently strongly under the influence of drink, and every now and then had to be steadied by the painted creature at his side. When he had seen them disappear up a narrow street, he walked hurriedly home like a man hardly awake. Fresh from the simple life of the country, his moral sense was shocked and outraged. In St. Iago drunkenness was looked upon as the parent of all vices, and he had been taught to regard it with utter loathing.

And this man was the friend of Ruby, and, for all he knew, her accepted lover.

"Oh, I would rather see her buried!" he said. "It is horrible—horrible! It cannot be—it must not be!" Then he paused and looked up at the stars. "Alas!" he said, in a tone of despair, "I am powerless to prevent it! If it is to be it will be!"

CHAPTER XIV

NOTICE TO QUIT

"The cloud of my perplexity
Grows denser every day."

WHEN Justin awoke next morning, he was half disposed to think that the experience of the night before was an unpleasant dream. He knew that Phil made no profession of religion, but that he was addicted to drink and to the vices that too often follow such indulgence was almost too painful to be believed.

"At any rate," he reflected, "I will keep the matter to myself until I have had further evidence. It may have been a sudden fall, and may never occur again."

Meanwhile, Justin found it almost impossible to put the matter entirely out of his thoughts. It made him suspicious, watchful, and uneasy. He had no idea of spying on his cousin; and yet, unconsciously having got on a certain trail, he followed it up. This was much easier than would appear at first sight. London is not so big, after all, and men move in comparatively small circles.

Within a month of that accidental meeting in the Strand, it was a matter of absolute certainty to Justin that Phil was a sharper and a rake. Even the firm of Mead, Runcorn, and Jago, brokers and commission agents, was only a blind, and, in some instances, a decoy. Mr. Phil Passmore in Regent's Park, was Mr. Jago to such as frequented No. 92, Melton Friars.

The revelation to Justin was altogether sickening; yet what could he do? Phil was his cousin. Should he go and openly denounce him? To whom? Who cared? If Phil Passmore, or a thousand Phil Passmore's, chose to waste their substance in riotous living, who was to hinder them? Did not one big section of London live on the follies of the rakes and fools who were in it?

Suppose he denounced him—what then? Phil was too much a man-about-town not to have an answer. To play shuttle-cock with a man's reputation was a very risky business, and might land him in gaol before he knew what had happened.

But the Lovedays ought to know. No doubt they ought. Perhaps they did know. But fashionable society did not trouble itself much

about such things. Men often got light-headed
and hilarious over dinner, and no one thought
the worse of them.

But—but——

Oh, well, such " buts " were not considered.
Young men were expected to sow their wild
oats, and no one was supposed to ask any
questions. Justin was not slow-witted, and it
was impossible to live in a big business house
in the heart of the city without learning a
hundred things that were a sealed book to him
before.

In Trelford everybody knew everybody else.
There were very few secrets in it. Nobody
could take an office without everybody being
acquainted with the fact, and without everybody
knowing also the character of the business he
did. In fact, people had so much time at their
disposal that they could not only attend to their
own affairs but to the affairs of everybody else.
That was one of the charms of living in a place
like Trelford. Nobody could feel alone there
or forsaken. Everybody took a kind of paternal
interest in all the rest. If you bought a new
umbrella, it was known, and also how much
you paid for it. If you sneezed twice, it was
matter for common remark before evening.

But in Cheapside Justin quickly realized the
contrast.

Once he asked the question, " Who occupies the offices on the next floor ?" and was politely told that he had better go and inquire. The city man does not know who his neighbour is, and, what is more, he does not care. He is so busy with his own concerns that he has no time to think about other people's.

Justin worried himself a great deal about Phil, but he appeared to be the only one who did so. And yet, if the truth must be told, it was not Phil's moral peril that was the chief cause of his anxiety—it was the thought of this unredeemed *roué* becoming the husband of Ruby Loveday. The prospect was bitter enough to contemplate when he believed that Phil was worthy of her, but now that he knew he was absolutely unworthy, it was positive torture.

He did not call on the Lovedays again for some weeks. He was terribly afraid of over-reaching his welcome. He did, however, go to the church they attended every Sunday morning. Not that he was impressed by the service or the preacher. In fact, he liked neither ; but he caught a glimpse of Ruby, and that was more to him just then than any sermon preached in London.

On the first Sunday he went very early, and inquired of the sexton where the Lovedays sat,

L

then he took a seat behind a pillar, where he could see with very little chance of being seen.

Ruby, in her devout Sunday attitude, seemed more bewitching than ever. To her the service was evidently no meaningless form; she entered into the spirit of it, and found in it real joy and inspiration. And as Justin sat and watched her pure, thoughtful face, and then contemplated the possibility of her marrying Phil Passmore, he grew sick at heart.

But what could he do? The old question was constantly cropping up. He could not tell Ruby. He could not soil her ears with such a narrative. And if he told Mr. Loveday would he be believed? Phil was evidently a friend of the family, and his word would be taken first; and if he denied it, as he doubtless would, then he would be discredited, and perhaps forbidden the house.

Moreover, it is not always easy to prove what you know to be facts, and to speak evil of one's own relatives is a sorry business at the best.

"I can do nothing," he would say to himself, bitterly. "If I were to breathe a word he would have me up for slander. My motives would be impugned, and I should be regarded as a sneak and a traitor."

So the days and weeks passed slowly away, and he found what comfort he could in watching Ruby from behind the pillar. Those were the only moments of sunshine in his dull, colourless life. In the city every day seemed like every other. The same weary routine had to be gone through, and he saw no hope of change or improvement.

He had come to London to make his fortune, and he was no nearer the realization of his hopes than at the start. Talk about there being no scope in Trelford. What scope was there shut up as an assistant in one department of a big city house? He might remain till he was grey, and blind, and bald, and still be serving behind the same counter.

Often enough in his duller moments he called himself a fool for ever leaving home, and a bigger fool for giving a second thought to Ruby Loveday.

"Why should I worry myself?" he would say to himself, angrily. "She can never be anything to me; and whether she marries Phil or somebody else, what can it matter? If she does not get him for a husband she may get somebody a great deal worse. But in any case I am out of it."

But the stern deductions of logic are never of any account to the young man who is in love.

He deliberately closes his eyes to facts, and goes steadily on, believing all things, hoping all things, enduring all things.

One Sunday morning in May, the weather being lovely, Justin, instead of returning to the city after church, got lunch at a small restaurant in the neighbourhood, and then sauntered back again into the Park. It was very delightful to hear the birds sing and feel the soft breath of the wind and smell the thousand perfumes that were floating about. As the afternoon wore away all the chairs got occupied, and crowds of people sauntered under the trees, and evidently enjoyed the balmy air. Among the rest came Ruby Loveday, on her way back from a mission-room, where she had been teaching a Sunday School class.

Justin was looking absently across the great stretch of park thinking of home, when Ruby paused in front of him and smiled. Instantly he looked up and their eyes met.

If it was spring-time before, it was summer now. Ruby was always gracious with him.

"You have come out to enjoy the spring sunshine?" she questioned.

"I have, Miss Loveday. Besides, all this great stretch of green makes me think of home."

"Then you still love the country?"

"Yes; I think I love it more than ever."

"But when people want to make their fortunes——" she said, with a mischievous twinkle
in her eyes.

"Please do not make fun of me," he answered, interrupting her, "for I have discovered that even in London fortune is only for
the few."

Suddenly her face grew grave. She did not
like to ask what he was doing, or how he was
succeeding, though she was very curious to
know. This grave-faced young Cornishman
interested her more than she knew. She often
found herself speculating on his chances of
success; and if her good wishes could have
helped him, his future would have been assured.

"You will come home and have tea with
us?" she said at length.

"It is very kind of you——" he began.

"No; please do not begin to invent an
excuse," she interrupted, with a laugh. "I am
sure father would be quite disappointed if he
knew you were so near and did not call."

"It is always a pleasure for me to call," he
answered, frankly; "only I don't like intruding
upon people on a Sunday."

"Then it is settled!" she said, gaily; and
they walked away together.

But the walk extended much farther than

they anticipated. They began to talk about Endilloe, and both grew so interested that he was bold enough to suggest that they should take another turn round a portion of the Park; and as Ruby raised no objection, the walk and the talk lengthened out and out.

That was a red-letter day in Justin's life. He often looked back to it in the dull and dismal days that followed, and tried to live it over again.

As they drew near the house, they caught sight of Phil Passmore standing at the drawing-room window watching them. Justin instinctively turned and looked at Ruby, and he saw the warm colour mount quickly to her neck and face. What did it mean? Was Phil her lover? And, if not, why did she blush at sight of him?

Phil was all smiles to Ruby, and she blushed again when he came to meet her. But Justin had never known him so frigid. But that might be partly his own fault, for he had grown so to despise his cousin that he could hardly help showing it.

Soon after tea Justin rose to go. He felt less free than he had done before; and somehow conversation flagged, and no one seemed entirely at his ease.

Phil rose at the same time, and, strangely

enough, no one asked either of them to stay. They passed out of the door side by side, and walked away down the street together. For awhile they walked on in silence, then Phil cleared his voice and spoke.

"You have scarcely been as frank with me, Justin, as I should have expected," he said, quietly.

"No?"

"Of course, I don't want to complain," he said, in an off-hand manner; "but, seeing I am your cousin, I hardly expected that you would try to hide from me the fact that you had taken a situation here."

"I was anxious not to bother any one with my affairs."

"Oh, that is all stuff and nonsense! Friends, and especially relatives, should be perfectly open and frank with each other."

"Do you think so?"

"I do. And to prove it, I want to tell you a bit of very interesting news."

"Indeed."

"Well it is interesting to me. The truth is, it is now practically settled that Ruby Loveday and myself become engaged."

"Is that so?" Justin questioned, with a gasp.

"It is, my boy. It will be publicly announced

in a very few days. Why don't you congratulate me?"

For a few moments Justin breathed hard, then he looked up and said, in a hard, unnatural voice—

"You wanted me to be perfectly frank with you?"

"Exactly. Why shouldn't you be?"

"Then may I ask first if she knows what you are?"

"What I am?"

"Yes. Have you told her the kind of life you lead? Have you told her that you get drunk? that you are a gambler and a libertine?"

Phil stopped suddenly short, and clenched his fists.

"Good heavens!" he said. "What do you mean?"

"I am being perfectly frank with you," was the slow and deliberate answer. "I have seen you drunk in the streets; seen you in company that no pure-minded man could be in. I have discovered something of the kind of life you are living in London, and I am ashamed of you. And for a man like you to even think of marrying a girl like Ruby Loveday is a sin and a crime in the sight of Heaven."

"So ho! A new Solomon come to judgment;" and Phil laughed cynically.

"And you are not ashamed of yourself?" he questioned, with flashing eyes.

"My poor, innocent cousin!" and Phil laughed again. "Well, really, I did not think you were quite so green. Suppose I go out to dinner, and get a little top-heavy—what then? And suppose, after dinner, I get into company that you with your prudish notions don't approve—what then? It's what every young fellow does."

"It's a lie!" Justin roared. "There are thousands of young men in London who are as pure-minded as all young men ought to be."

"Pah!—shop-assistants! molly-coddlers from the country! Y.M.C.A. young men! I am not talking about milk-sops, but about men."

"Men, indeed!" Justin said, scornfully. "And do you mean to tell me that Ruby Loveday knows that you are of this type?"

"Of course she does, you innocent!" and he laughed again. "Do you think any girl of grit would want a molly-coddle?"

"Then God help her!" he said, bitterly; and turning suddenly on his heel, he strode off in the opposite direction.

On the following Saturday, when he went for his month's pay, he received two months' instead, and was informed by his employer that his services were no longer required.

CHAPTER XV

ADRIFT

"A fathomless sea is rolling
O'er the wreck of my bravest bark."

JUSTIN took his dismissal very philosophically. He was surprised, of course, that he should be dismissed without warning, and practically without explanation. Why, if it was simply a case of shortening hands, should he have been given a month's wages in lieu of notice? There was evidently more beneath the surface than he could see; and, strangely enough, no suspicion of the truth crossed his mind. He never once thought of connecting Phil Passmore with his loss of situation.

On the whole, he was rather pleased than otherwise to be adrift. He was convinced that along the humdrum way of salaried service there was no chance of making a fortune. Now that he was tied to no particular place and might turn his attention to the first likely thing that offered, Dame Fortune might condescend to smile upon him. So he secured cheap lodgings near King's Cross, and went out to explore London, and by the end of a month he had pretty well mastered its geography, though he had done nothing else of any practical value.

But for his pride he would have gone back to Endilloe; for he was utterly sick of the great city, and was pining for the rest and quiet of the green fields and a sight of the glorious sea. But how could he go back and confess himself a failure? What explanation could he give of his sudden dismissal? No, no. He was in London, and would have to remain there, though he hated it with all his heart.

He did not call again on the Lovedays. After his last experience, he had a feeling that he was not wanted. Nevertheless, he often found his way into Regent's Park, and hoped and almost prayed that he might see Ruby. Twice from behind his pillar in the church he had feasted his eyes upon her face, but that was not enough. He wanted to walk with her and talk with her under the trees. He wanted to make sure that Phil had told him the truth.

But for all his watching and waiting, Ruby did not come near him, and when in desperation he passed and repassed the house and stared up at the windows, she did not show her face, and he had not the courage to pull at the door-bell.

He was equally unsuccessful in his endeavours to find his cousin. He went several times to Melton Friars; but the office-boy was always the only occupant, and he appeared to know absolutely nothing as to the movements of the heads of the firm. Misfortune was breaking down Justin's pride very considerably, and he was quite prepared to ask Phil's pardon for plain speaking, and to solicit his aid in getting another situation.

But Phil was not to be found; and Justin was forced to the conclusion at last that he kept out of his way of set purpose. Then he tried to find Mr. Loveday's city address; but in this he was entirely unsuccessful. So after six weeks of tramping the streets of London, he resolved to appeal to Mr. Loveday in his home.

It was with very mixed feelings that he pulled at the bell and waited for the door to open. He remembered that they had not been to church for the last two Sundays, so possibly some one was ill. The door was opened at length, and he was informed by a strange servant that the family was out of town.

"Will they be back soon?" he questioned.

"No; not for several weeks yet."

"Thank you." And he descended the steps with a strange sinking at his heart.

"I expect it is true," he said to himself. "As

the accepted lover of Ruby, Phil has gone with them."

He walked away in the direction of Marylebone Road with his eyes bent upon the ground. "What am I to do now?" was the question he repeated to himself over and over again. For six weeks he had waited on fortune, but without success. Fortune had her favourites, and evidently he was not one of them. He might have known that, if he had only taken the trouble to think. Fortune had never favoured the Pentyres. They had been its football for generations.

"Oh, I wish I had never come to this horrid place," he muttered to himself. "I was a fool to think there was a better chance for me here than at home, and now I am paying for my folly."

He was in a very depressed mood when he sought the shelter of his lodgings that evening. The glare and noise of the streets almost made him sick. The weather was hot and oppressive; beautiful June sunshine lay upon the land, but it seemed to make London all the more ugly and intolerable.

He stole up to his stuffy little bed- and sitting-room combined, and gave himself up to dreams of home. He pictured Dorothy out in the cool orchard dreaming over her knitting. He saw his mother bustling in and out of the kitchen. He

heard the bleating of the lambs in the distant
meadows, and saw the fir-trees glow in the light
of the setting sun. He felt the wind from the
wide Atlantic cooling his hot brow, and heard
the deep boom of the waves as they broke upon
the shore. And from the long stretch of Downs
came the perfume of heather and gorse, mingling
with the more pungent odour from the pine-
trees.

And he had left all this for noisy, sweltering
London!

"What a fool I have been!" he muttered to
himself, bitterly. "I should have been better off
if I had remained at home."

But the old question came back again:
"What am I to do now?"

His small hoard of money was rapidly
running out. His clothes were getting the
worse for wear, and Ruby was more utterly lost
to him than ever.

If he could have gone back to Endilloe on
any reasonable pretext, he would have turned
his back on London for ever; but he had no
excuse that would satisfy the inquisitive people
of St. Iago. They would worm out the truth
before he had been at home twenty-four hours.

For the same reason, he could not write to
his old employer for a fresh reference. In
truth, he was utterly stranded; and unless his

luck turned, he might sink down to the level of a sandwich man.

He saw also that he had made a mistake in keeping himself so much aloof from his fellows. He had joined no church, no debating society, no club, no association of any kind; consequently he was without friends or advisers.

On the following day he sought an interview with his old foreman, and laid his whole case before him.

The foreman took him aside into his little room, and shutting the door with a snick, said—

"Look here, Pentyre. What was at the back of your leaving Cornwall?"

"At the back?" Justin questioned, in astonishment.

"Yes. I mean, what compelled you to leave? What scrape had you been getting into? I would like to get to the bottom of it, if I could."

"I really don't know what you mean," Justin said, with a look of bewilderment in his eyes. "I got into no scrape at all. Weren't my references satisfactory?"

"I believe they were excellent, and that makes it all the more puzzling; and yet I have been given to understand that there were some reasons that made it advisable that you should leave."

"But who gave you to understand any such

thing?" Justin asked, his eyes blazing. "I left because, like a fool, I thought I should stand a better chance of improving my position here than at home."

"Then may I ask if you have any enemies in London, or is it to any one's advantage that you should not get on?"

"Not that I am aware of. I scarcely know a soul in the place."

"But you do know a few, of course?"

"I know a Mr. Loveday slightly, and I know my cousin Phil, of course. He's something in the city—I really don't know what."

"Your cousin, of course, would like you to get on. At least, I presume there is no reason why he should object to your getting on?"

"Object to my getting on?" he questioned, bringing out the words slowly, as though a new idea was just dawning upon his mind. "Well, now you mention it, he might object. Why do you ask?"

"First, let me ask what this cousin of yours is like."

Justin described him to the minutest detail.

"H'm, it looks fishy!" was the reply.

"But what do you know about him?" Justin asked, anxiously.

"Nothing. Only, a few days before you were cashiered, the governor was interviewed by a

M

smart, well-dressed gentleman. What he said, I don't know. The governor is a reticent man. But from hints, the governor was warned against you, and he was evidently not willing to take the risk of keeping you beyond the week-end."

"And you think my cousin is at the root of the mischief?"

"All I can say is that your description of him tallies exactly with the man who interviewed the governor."

"The scoundrel!" Justin muttered, with clenched hands. "I see it all now. Heavens! if I had not been so slow-witted, I might have seen it all weeks ago."

"Wouldn't you do wisely, Pentyre, to go back home again? It's awkward for a young fellow to be on the loose in a place like London."

"I can't go back, Mr. Brown, under present circumstances," was the reply. "How can I confess that I have been defeated, that I was dismissed from my situation? Why, I should never be able to hold up my head again."

"It's awkward, certainly, but it's better than starving here."

"I don't know about that. I think, on the whole, I'd rather starve. But I needn't starve, if somebody will only give me a start. I'm not afraid of work; and if I'm to begin at the bottom, then so be it."

"I suppose you wouldn't like to go into the warehouse?" Mr. Brown said, reflectively.

"And do porter's work?"

"Well, it amounts to that. There's a vacancy just now, and the governor might be inclined to consider you. I believe he regrets acting so hastily."

"I'll go into the warehouse with pleasure," Justin said, "if the governor will only give me a chance."

"Well, come again to-morrow morning, and in the meantime I will do the best I can for you."

So Justin went out again into the crowded street and into the summer sunshine, feeling much more hopeful than he had done for weeks past.

"Now," he reflected, "I will make another effort to find that cousin of mine. And if I am successful he will remember it."

He was not successful, however. No. 92, Melton Friars was where it had always been, but a new plate was on the door, and a new name across the window. What had become of Mead, Runcorn, and Jago no one knew, and to all appearances no one cared.

Justin spent the whole day in making inquiries and hunting up directories, but he was a novice at the task, and so all his efforts ended in failure. The more Justin tried to explore the city proper the more perplexed he grew and the more mysterious it appeared to him.

What did all these people do? How did they make a living? If a man owned a shop or a warehouse the thing seemed straightforward enough; but thousands and tens of thousands of these people seemed to have only offices— offices in narrow courts, in dingy alleys, in curious *culs-de-sac;* offices in cellars and up half a dozen flights of stairs; offices palatial and offices mean, but what these offices stood for the novice did not know and could not even guess.

Justin went back to his lodgings that night tired, but still hopeful. That he was the victim of his cousin's hate and jealousy he had no doubt; but that was better than being Fortune's football. He could localize the evil now, put his finger on the exact spot, work along the line from effect to cause, and he had an unfaltering belief in the just government of the world.

If he were suffering merely from his own folly or stupidity Providence might leave him to his fate; but since he was the victim of the malice and wickedness of another there was a chance for him. In the long run villainy worked its own destruction and honest men came into their own.

"Perhaps I shall win yet," he said to himself. "I shall have to begin lower down—perhaps at the bottom. I shall have to pocket my pride and be content to be simply a working man. Well, anything is better than utter failure."

The next morning he was stirring early. He felt that he had reached a crisis in his life.

CHAPTER XVI

"The dearest spot on earth to me
Is home, sweet home."

On the following Monday morning Justin made
a fresh start. It was not without a sense of
the irony of life that he exchanged his broad-
cloth for much coarser material; but he tried
to comfort himself with the reflection that he
would be almost as well off wheeling trucks
in the warehouse as he would waiting upon
customers in the show-rooms. But in any
case he was too thankful for the chance of earning his bread to grumble at anything. So he
neatly folded his frock-coat suits and put them
away. He might want them occasionally on
Sundays if he found himself in the humour to
go to church, but on other days a cloth cap
and heavy boots would bear evidence of his
social grade.

For several Sundays he felt too tired to go

anywhere, but, try as he would, he could not crush the longing to see Ruby. She might be the promised wife of his cousin; that did not matter. Until the fatal knot was tied he would feast his eyes on her now and then if he could get anywhere within sight of her.

So one hot Sunday morning in July he climbed to the top of an omnibus, and was borne westward once more. As usual, he was early at the church, and so made for his favourite seat behind the pillar. He waited very impatiently for the service to begin, for the Lovedays rarely put in an appearance till the last minute. One after another the worshippers came in and took their seats, but he kept his eyes on one pew which still remained empty. At last the service began, and still they had not arrived. One after another the empty pews were filled by strangers.

"Ah! here they are at last;" and his heart gave a sudden throb.

But why was the sexton showing them to their pew? A second glance and the light faded out of his eyes. They were not the Lovedays!

The service seemed interminable that morning, and he could have sworn that the sermon was an hour long. He sat as still as he could, in a spirit of grim endurance, and when at length the benediction was pronounced, he seized his hat and was out of the church like a flash.

To walk past the Lovedays' house would not be at all out of his way. He must inquire again. They surely could not be still out of town. Perhaps some one was ill.

He hurried on at a rapid pace until he stood before the well-known door. Surely he had mistaken the terrace or the number. He walked past some distance, then back again. No; it was the same house, but empty. "To be let," stared at him from the dining-room windows.

His heart sank like lead. Where had they gone to? Why had they gone? What had happened? Alas! a hundred things might have happened. More than two months had passed since he had seen any of them, and they might have gone to the ends of the earth in that time.

Justin returned to his lodgings on foot, and for the rest of the day did not venture out of the house.

During the next six months nothing happened to disturb the monotony of Justin's life. Every day was like every other day, the same weary round of toil without change or variation. He did his work well, but he got no advancement either in position or pay. At the week-end he received his wages, but nothing was said to him either in the way of praise or blame. He kept hoping, as he had hoped ever since he came to London, that Fortune would find him out and smile upon him, but hitherto she had not come his way.

He did his best to find out the whereabouts of the Lovedays, but without success. Nor did he get a sight of his cousin Phil, though he was always on the watch for him when he was out-of-doors.

Every week he got a long letter from Dorothy, telling him all the news of St. Iago. It was not much, but it was intensely welcome. It made him forget for the moment his dreary surroundings. It brought back to him vividly the scenes that he would never cease to love.

Dorothy was always cheerful. She never referred to her truant lover or to her long-deferred hopes. She might have been far more concerned at Ruby's long silence, and nearly every letter she asked Justin "If it were not possible for him to find out what had become of the Lovedays."

Towards the end of January, however, she wrote that it was rumoured in St. Iago that Phil and Ruby had been married very quietly, and had gone to the South of France to spend their honeymoon. The following week she wrote again and said that there could be very little doubt the rumour was true, as a paragraph to the same effect had appeared in the *West Briton.* So week by week fresh items of news were added. One was that Phil had made a big fortune by speculation; another that Mr. Loveday had suffered very serious reverses. A third was that Ruby had married Phil to save her father's credit, and a fourth that Mr. Loveday had opposed the match and that Ruby had taken the law into her own hands and run off with her lover. Later rumours stated that Mr. Loveday was in very precarious health, and that he had hastened the wedding so that he might see Ruby comfortably settled in life before he died.

But contradictory and improbable as some of these reports were, the fatal item that Ruby and Phil were married appeared in all. At first Justin refused to believe any of them, and steadily hoped against hope; but the rumours became so persistent and circumstantial that at length he was no longer able to hold out against them.

"I have been a fool," he said to himself, bitterly, "to hope at all. But this is the end of it;" and if he did not wholly succeed in tearing

Ruby's image from his heart it was not for want of trying.

For several weeks he never even donned his Sunday clothes. He was too utterly miserable to take interest in anything. If he could have slipped quietly out of life he would have been supremely thankful. The loss of Ruby seemed to blight every other hope. What had he to live for now? Was mere existence worth fighting for? He might struggle his way for fifty years as a labouring man and then end his days in a workhouse. Was that a prospect to be contemplated with any degree of satisfaction?

Moreover, he had loved Ruby with such reverence and tenderness. She had been his ideal of all womanly beauty and virtue. His affection had amounted almost to worship. Consequently, the shock of her marriage to such a rake as Phil Passmore absolutely staggered him. He could not bear to think of it. It was sacrilege in its basest form.

Then came another shock, and his life entered on a new phase. Getting home late one evening from his work, he found a letter awaiting him in his father's handwriting.

This was such a rare occurrence that he tore open the envelope at once, much wondering what had happened. He had not read many sentences before he dropped into a chair, while

a troubled and angry light came into his eyes.
The letter was as follows :—

"My dear Son,—I don't want to interfere in
any way with your prospects of getting on; but
it would be a great comfort to me just now
if you were at home.   Things don't go very
well, somehow, and it seems to me there is likely
to be worse troubles ahead.   Lord Tregeagle's
steward was round here the other day taking
stock of the dwelling-house and barns, and he
said there were some repairs that wanted doing,
and that I'd better get them done at once.   So
I up at once, and told him that it was no business of his, that as the houses were mine and
built on my own freehold, I should do the
repairs when I liked or let them alone; at
which he smiled knowingly, and said that, as far
as he was aware, I had not yet proved my title.
Well, at that I fired up, as you may think, and
asked him if Lord Tregeagle had proved his title
to the land he stole from the Pentyres.   Well, I
can't tell you all that passed between us—but
you may depend on it, neither mother nor I
slept much that night.   Well, next morning I
saddled Nero, and rode over to Trelford to see
Lawyer Nankivel.   He looked surprised to see
me, for you know I never have anything to do
with lawyers if I can help it.   So I told him at

once that I'd come to have a look at the Endilloe deeds. He looked surprised at that, and then I began to tell him what old Bice, the steward, had been saying the day before. But in the end he told me that he hadn't got the deeds. 'But I always understood my father to say they were kept in your office,' I said. But he assured me it wasn't so. Then he showed me heaps and heaps of deed-boxes, with the people's names painted on them; but there was no box belonging to the Pentyres. Then he brought out a big book, and showed me a list of names of people and estates; but there was no Pentyre or Endilloe in the list. Well, by this time I was in a great way, as you may be sure; and, in fact, I haven't got over it yet. I don't know what to do next. I can't find the deeds, and I daren't let anybody know they are missing. I made believe to Nankivel that I expected they were in our strong chest at home, but that I hadn't thought of looking—and no more I hadn't then—but I looked enough when I got home. But I fancy old Bice suspects something, for he was round here again yesterday, squinting up at the roof and examining the doors and windows. I had a mind to order him off the premises as a trespasser, and had I been a younger man, I'd have done it too, and given point to my argument with the toe of my boot; but when he saw

that I was looking, he walked off in a casual
kind of way. The old rascal means mischief:
you can see it in his eye. He's a sight worse
than his master, which is a pity, for a harder
landlord than Tregeagle I hope doesn't exist.
Then, to make matters worse, my 'take' in the
farm runs out at Midsummer; and I can get no
promise that the lease shall be renewed. So, all
things considered, I've reason for feeling anxious.
I don't know that you could do any good if you
were at home. But you're my only son, and
London seems a terrible long way off. Perhaps
I ought to feel more self-reliant as I get
older and more experienced; but I don't, somehow. Young heads are sometimes better than
old ones, and, in any case, two heads are better
than one. But don't let me persuade you, my
son. You have your living to get, and your way
to make in the world, and I hope you find that
easier in London than I have found it at home
here. Perhaps things will come out all right.
I hope they will, but I am very doubtful; and I
feel as if I wanted somebody to lean upon,
somebody stronger than myself. I hope you
are still doing well, and are comfortable in your
lodgings. We still miss you very much, particularly in the evenings. Your mother and
Dorothy keep very well. Dorothy is nearly
always cheerful, bless her. I reckon your

mother and I would mope ourselves to death but for Dorothy. It's rumoured down here that Phil Passmore has come into a big fortune through his wife, and that he's given up business, and lives in a big house in the country somewhere. I shouldn't like you, my boy, to miss any good fortune on my account. I expect I shall be able to struggle along somehow. Your mother and Dorothy join me in lots of love.

"Your affectionate father,

"JOHN PENTYRE."

When Justin had finished the letter he turned to the beginning and read it through a second time, and a gentler light came into his eyes as he did so, and now and then he smiled broadly. His father's allusions to his chances of getting on and making his fortune struck him as being absolutely comical.

"Poor old father!" he said to himself at length. "He little guesses what a sorry failure I am!"

For a long time he did not see the bare little room in which he sat, and was not conscious of the far-off roar of the streets. He was back again in Endilloe, listening to his father and mother while they discussed the new turn of events.

At length he started to his feet, while a bright, radiant look swept over his face.

"I must go home," he said, and he flung his cap against the ceiling, then kicked it to the other end of the room.

"It's an ill wind that doesn't blow good to somebody," he went on, "and this new turn of affairs gives me a chance of saying good-bye to London. Yes, I must go home—*home!* think of it;" and he sat down again and actually laughed.

"Oh, we'll manage somehow," he continued; "and if we're turned out of Endilloe, we'll find some other place. But we're not turned out yet, and we'll have a fight for it. Anyhow, we'll all be together again, and that's something."

He scarcely slept a wink that night. The thought of going home again intoxicated him. It seemed years since he left the dear old place for the untried life of the great city. Ah, with what high hopes he had entered it! How he had dreamt of winning his way to fortune, and then going to Ruby Loveday and laying it at her feet and asking for her love. What beautiful castles he had built in the air, in all of which Ruby had reigned as wife and queen.

Ah, well, he had had his romance, and seen the end of it. Mere worldly success was nothing to him now. It was all for the sake of Ruby that he wanted to get rich. Now that she was lost to him, nothing mattered very much. His first thought must be for his father and mother and Dorothy.

On the following morning he gave the usual notice to his employers, and a week later he packed up all his belongings and started for home.

N

CHAPTER XVII

A FAMILY COUNCIL

" We must not play the coward,
    Even though gain should lie that way."

IT was evening, and nearly dark, when he reached Endilloe. The day had been one of the longest he could remember. So impatient was he to reach home that he scarcely noticed the green mantle of spring with which Nature was clothing the hills and fields. Several times he tried to lose himself in the pages of a stirring novel that he brought with him; but reading was altogether out of the question. Nothing would have suited him so well as being stoker on the engine.

At last! at last! The train had scarcely stopped when he was out on the platform. He had seen his father, and was by his side in a moment.

" My boy, you look pale and thin," John said, with a pathetic shake in his voice.

"I have been working hard," was the quick reply.   "But how are you and the others?"

"We are all very well—that is, we are very well in health," was the somewhat dubious answer ; and then Justin's luggage claimed immediate attention.

In a few minutes they were driving along the quiet lanes in the direction of Endilloe. Justin's heart was too full for speech.   The very smell of the dear homeland was like a benediction to him.   The breezy April day was dying swiftly in the west ; the outlines of the hills were growing vague and indistinct.

"Everything looks very natural, father," he said at length, trying to keep out of his voice all trace of emotion.

"Well, it's getting too dark to see much, my boy," was the reply.   "But things don't change much down this way—at least, they don't in appearance."

Justin was quick to note the qualifying note in his father's words, but decided to wait for explanations.

Dorothy was at the garden gate when the trap drove up, and greeted her brother with a silent kiss.   She could not trust herself to speak just then.

At the open door stood the mother—a veritable Martha in her own house, cumbered about much serving. She kissed her son on both cheeks, and then held his face between her hands, and looked at him in silence.

There was an appetizing supper ready to be put on the table, and in a few minutes the little family circle was complete once more. Justin gave a long sigh when his father came in and took his seat and the door was shut.

"Oh, it is lovely to be home again!" he said. "One never knows how nice home is till one goes away."

"We have missed you terribly, Justin," Dorothy answered, without looking at him.

"And it seems years ago since you went away," said the mother.

John looked up as though he meant to say something and then thought better of it, and proceeded to attack his supper.

For awhile there was silence; then Mrs. Pentyre looked up and said—

"And have you come home for good, Justin?"

"I hope so, mother."

"But it will mean a great loss to you?" Dorothy questioned.

"That remains to be seen," he said, with a laugh. "And then, you know, Dorothy, money is not everything."

"And London is a terribly dear place to live in," Mrs. Pentyre interposed.

"There is no doubt about that, mother; but let's not talk about London now. What about Endilloe? Have there been any fresh developments lately?"

John laid down his knife and fork, and looked troubled.

"I thought we wouldn't talk about it," he said, "till we'd finished our supper."

"Then you have some fresh news?" he questioned.

"Yes, Justin, we have; but—— "

"Oh, never mind the 'but'!" he interrupted, with a laugh. "Let's have it at once! I can assure you I'm not going to let it spoil my appetite."

"Well, then, Justin, I'm afraid we shall have to leave here. Bice was round here again yesterday—— "

"Confound him!"

"Yes; we may confound him as much as we like, but I'm afraid he's got the whip-hand of us."

"Why so?"

"Because we've no papers, Justin."

"But what title has Lord Tregeagle?"

"Well, Bice says that he's absolute title, and that I and my father before me and his father and his—have all been living here on sufferance."

"Which statement you asked him to prove?"

"I did; and he produced a big map, coloured red——"

"Which embraced Endilloe, of course?"

"It did, my son."

Justin laughed. "It'll take a good deal of bluff of that kind to affect me," he said.

"What do you mean by bluff?" Dorothy questioned.

"I mean, Dorothy, that Bice and his master expect, no doubt, that if they only bluster, and show fight, and threaten, and make assertions loud enough, we shall yield, and they will be able to take undisturbed possession."

"But what can a poor man do," John interposed, pathetically, "when a great landlord drops down upon him in that way? A big magnate like Tregeagle has all the machinery of the nation at his back."

"I know all the odds are in his favour," Justin answered; "nevertheless, it would be cowardly to yield without a struggle. You are now about the only freeholder left in the parish, and Tregeagle wants to crush you out as he has crushed out all the others. But there's going to be a fight for it this time."

"I would not mind fighting," John said,

sadly, "if any good was likely to come out of it."

"No good can come of quietly yielding," Justin said, with spirit.

"I don't know about that," John replied. "Bice says that if I let the thing go without making a fuss, there is a chance that I may be allowed to have the farm again at the same rent."

"Did he say that?"

"Well, those are not his exact words, but he hinted at it plain enough. On the other hand, if I do resist, I shall be turned out of the farm, and in the end, I fear, shall lose Endilloe into the bargain."

"Oh, I see. Well, they are playing a pretty deep game; but it isn't going to answer this time."

John shook his head.

"No, father. You have sent for me and I have come home, but I have not come home to yield up my life at the bidding of the agent of Lord Tregeagle. I have come home to fight this thing out, and I intend to do it to the last drop of my blood."

Dorothy's nostrils dilated and her eyes sparkled, but she did not say anything just then.

"But there is another side to the question,

my son," John said, after a pause. "If Endilloe
really does belong to Lord Tregeagle, as Mr.
Bice says it does, why——"

"Please let us not discuss that 'if,' father,"
Justin interrupted, hastily. "Endilloe has
belonged to the Pentyres for generations."

"But Lord Tregeagle is an honourable man,
and he evidently believes that Endilloe belongs
to him."

"Very likely he does. Men of his class
generally believe that everything belongs to
them that they can lay hands on."

"Well, and when things are sifted to the
bottom, it is generally found that they are right.
They own nearly all the land of England."

"Quite true," Justin said, with a cynical
smile.

"Well, look at Winterdown Common as a
case in point," John went on. "There were
three hundred acres of it, and it had been looked
upon as common land for generations. Everybody that liked turned out his cows and sheep
and donkeys on it. But it was shown, in the end,
that nobody had any right to do it. The land all
the while belonged to Lord Tregeagle and Lord
Fortyways, and ten years ago, as you may
remember, they divided it equally between
them; and it is now let out in small farms which
bring them in a good rent."

"Exactly," Justin answered; "and the same story may be told in nearly every parish in England. A hundred years ago there was some common land in England that belonged to the people. There was a green in every village where the children had a right to play. But that day is over. Nearly every acre of common land has been filched from the people and added to the estates of the rich."

"No; do not say 'filched,' Justin. You might as well say that they have stolen the land."

"Exactly. I do not mind which word you use, either will suit me."

"But they don't suit me, my son. You can't object to people claiming their rights."

"Rights, father?" he said, slowly and bitterly. "They have grown up—have been cradled in the belief, in fact, that only they have rights, and that the poor people have no rights at all. We have been robbed and oppressed for centuries."

"No, no; that is wild, Radical talk, and I hate it. I believe in the old ways, and the old laws, and the old constitution, and we are taught to render respect to our betters."

"Oh yes," Justin said, impatiently. "I will render respect to any man who is deserving of respect. But when a man tries to rob me, then I will resist him to the last gasp."

"I don't blame you for feeling strongly," John replied, slowly. "I felt just as bitter myself when old Bice first came sneaking round here. But when he assured me yesterday that Lord Tregeagle's title was good, and that he'd been generous all these years in not enforcing it, what could I do?"

"You could have given him the lie to his face. As it is, he will assume that you have lost, or mislaid, the deeds, and so will become all the more arrogant in consequence."

"Oh, well, Justin, I'm not a fighting man, as you know, and I'm awfully glad you've come home, for I've been at my wits' end."

"And will you leave the matter now in my hands?"

"Well, Justin;" and John shook his head slowly from side to side, "it's this way: you never would be a farmer, and there is nothing else that I can do. And if I'm turned out from here, what's to become of me?"

Justin dropped his head, and for some time ate in silence. His father seemed bent on giving away the whole case, and if he was going to remain in that mood there was no use in attempting anything. He would be like a man fighting with his hands tied.

Dorothy was watching him intently. She could read his face like a book, and she dreaded lest he should say that he would give up the whole contention, and go away again. For herself, she believed in resisting to the last. The Pentyres in the past had been much too yielding, and consequently had lost nearly all their possessions. It was time that some one came who had strength to resist. She spoke up at last.

"Are you forgetting those who will come after you, father?" she inquired.

John started, and looked at her for a moment in silence.

"I'm afraid I have been forgetting," he said at length. "Yes, it's a very proper question."

Justin's brow cleared at once, and he looked across the table at Dorothy and smiled. John did not speak again for some time, then he turned to Justin.

"Endilloe is as much yours as mine," he said, slowly. "I was forgetting that. And if you like to fight for it I'm not going to stand in the way. But I'm afraid it will be a losing game, my son. You see, we've no papers."

"Possession is nine points of the law," Justin said, with a laugh, "and we'll bluff the tenth."

"Bluffing may do with a man your own size," John answered, pathetically. "But think of Lord Tregeagle's purse, and influence, and

position.   Besides, he has the whole House of
Lords at his back."

"Yes, I know all that," Justin said, bitterly,
"And I don't know that I have any real hope
of winning.   It is not often, it seems to me.
that the Pentyres have been on the winning
side; but, at any rate, there will be the satisfaction of resisting wrong and oppression.   In
a fight of this kind the poor man has scarcely
a chance, I know.   But he need not play the
coward on that account.   I would a thousand
times rather die fighting for the right than yield
to the wrong and live."

"Very good, my son," John said, with a little
sigh.   "Then we shall have our answer ready
when Mr. Bice calls to-morrow."   ·

"Leave Mr. Bice to me," Justin said, smiling.
"I have often ached to have a word with that
gentleman."

So the little family council settled the matter,
and waited rather impatiently for the coming
day.

CHAPTER XVIII

PREPARING FOR ACTION

"I have set my life upon a cast,
    And I will stand the hazard of the die."

LONG before noon on the following day, everybody in St. Iago knew that Justin was back
again from London, and most people had a
fairly shrewd guess as to the reasons that
had brought him home. It was known that
John Pentyre's "take" ran out at Midsummer,
and that Mr. Bice had given the farmer no
promise that it should be renewed. It had also
got whispered abroad that Lord Tregeagle had
been claiming, through his agent, Endilloe House
with its gardens, orchard, and twenty acres of
meadow land, and that it was doubtful if John
Pentyre had any legal title to the place.

Nor was that all. It was believed that Lord
Tregeagle was all-powerful in the county, and
that it was useless for any poor man to pit his
strength against him. Hence, if he had cast
covetous eyes on John's little bit of freehold,

that freehold would be his, and John Pentyre
would resist and wriggle in vain.

Of course, everybody sympathized with John
in this new calamity. There was something
pathetic in the sight of this ancient and once
flourishing family being reduced to the level of
the common herd ; but it had been the fate of
nearly every small freeholder in the parish.
For some reason or other the big estates had
grown, and the small estates had dwindled ;
and the case of Endilloe was evidently going
to be a repetition of several others.

"I reckon Maister Justin be a-comed home
from up London Churchtown for to stop old
Bice from gobbling up Endilloe," Amos Blue
said to Nathan Hendy on the morning after
Justin's return. "But he might as well try to
stop the tide from coming in down to Poldula
porth, that's what I do say."

"I'm glad he's come home, all the same,"
Nathan replied. "It's wastin' a good life to
live in thews big towns; the folks be that
ignorant."

"I don't know 'bout that," Amos said reflectively. "Ef it be as you say, why be folks
always crackin' up London and the folks as
lives there ?"

"Pure ignorance," said Nathan, with energy.
"They don't know no better, that's the reason.

Look at old Bice; he ain't never lived in no
big town, and see what he knows. He could
tie knots in any Londoner as ever was. He
can make black white wi' just winkin', an' can
write lies on paper as looks so much like truth
that nobody could tell the difference. He means
to gobble up Endilloe; an' I agree wi' you,
Amos, as he's going to do it."

"But if the maister have the papers all in
proper order?" questioned Amos, as if anxious
to hope even against hope.

"I've thought of that too," said Nathan;
"but, lor', when old Bice makes up his mind
to a thing, it's all up. You see, he's Lord
Tregeagle at his back, and all the rest of the
big-wigs, an' they all hang together like a string
of onions."

"But it's hard on the poor folks," said
Amos.

"Ay, but it's our lot," Nathan said, with a
sigh. "Providence, I suppose, meaned it to be
so; so 'taint no use complainin'."

"I don't know," said Amos. "If I'd anything to fight for—which I ain't—I do believe
as how I'd kick out to the last. An' I hope
as how Mr. Justin 'll show fight in this case."

"I'm afraid as how living up in that big
town have spoilt 'im," Nathan remarked, with
a grunt, and walked away.

Meanwhile, Justin and Dorothy were discussing the situation over a late breakfast. Mrs. Pentyre was busy in the dairy, and John was superintending affairs on the farm.

"Oh, Justin," Dorothy had said, "I cannot tell you how delighted I am to see you home again; but I have been wondering all the night what you will do now you are at home."

"Never fear, Dorothy," he answered, brightly; "I shall be able to get my bread somehow. But my first business will be to find the Endilloe deeds, and checkmate old Bice."

"And suppose you fail? Suppose the deeds are irretrievably lost—what then? Father and mother have searched everywhere, and they have both given up hope."

"Of course, if we are ejected from Endilloe we shall have to find some other place."

"It will nearly break father's heart."

"That is all the more reason why I should stand by him. We might take a smaller place than this, and the two of us might do the work."

"But you hate farming, Justin."

"No; it is the conditions under which we groan that I hate, though I admit I should never take up farming from choice."

"I wish I knew how I could earn something," Dorothy said, with a sigh. "There seems no chance for women in this world."

"Unless they go out as domestic servants," Justin answered, with a laugh. "Then they have it all their own way."

"Do you think I might succeed in that line?" Dorothy questioned, looking up at him.

"You might, if you could pocket the family pride."

"Would you like me to make the attempt?"

"No, Dorothy; while I am able to keep a roof over my head, there will always be a home for you."

She turned away her eyes from him, and looked out of the window, and he fancied he saw the glisten of a tear-drop on her lids. For awhile neither spoke again. Then he said abruptly—

"Do you ever hear from Tom Pendarvis now?"

She started, and a hot blush swept over her face.

"No, Justin.   Why do you ask?"

"I hardly know," he said, hesitatingly. "Curiosity, I expect."

"I keep hoping every day," she replied, the colour fading slowly from her face, "that I shall hear from him."

"Then you believe in him still?"

"I have had no reason for doubting him," was the quick reply.

o

"But it is more than three years ago since he went away."

"If he keeps silence for thrice three years I shall still believe in him."

Justin sighed, but he asked no more questions just then. He had no wish to cast a single shadow across Dorothy's hope. Let her cherish it as long as she could. His had gone out in darkness all too soon.

It seemed only yesterday since he had sat in that very room, and built the most romantic castles that any one had ever seen. He would go to London. He would seize Dame Fortune by the hand directly on his arrival. He would rise more rapidly in the commercial world than Dick Whittington of old. He would show not only his Cornish friends, but all London, what energy, and honesty, and enterprise could accomplish, and then he would offer his hand and his fortune to Ruby Loveday, and she would crown his life with her love to the end of his days.

He was glad now that he had never taken any one into his confidence. To what an inglorious end his hope and striving had come! How miserably all his schemes had failed! How absolutely wasted had been the treasure of his love!

No doubt a similar fate was in store for

Dorothy, but he would not tell her so. Let her go on loving and hoping. Hope enriched, though it went out in darkness, and Love ennobled the life though it might never be returned. It was not by being loved that the heart was purified, but by loving.

Breakfast finished, Justin put on his hat and went out into the spring sunshine. How wide the world seemed after the London streets! How sweet and strong the air that blew in from the sea! How absolutely unfettered he felt! He wanted to run and jump and shout; and had he been certain that no one would have seen or heard him, he would have done so.

Down in one of the fields he came across Amos digging out a ditch. Amos straightened his back with unusual alacrity and waited for Justin to come up.

"I be purty an' glad to see 'ee, Maister Justin," he said, eagerly, breaking in upon Justin's friendly "Good morning." "Terrible glad I be, and there's no denyin' it. I only wish I could see our Dan'l 'ome from the same place."

"Daniel is still in London, is he?" Justin questioned, with a smile.

"Oah, iss. Dedn'ee never see 'im all the time you was up in that there town, now?"

"No, I never once caught sight of him. I looked out for him, of course."

"'Tes terrible strange," Amos said, reflectively. "'Ome here to St. Iago people do get to knaw each other terrible quick."

"But you see London is a much bigger place."

"Iss, iss, so they do say. But ded 'ee ever ax for our Dan'l when you was up there?"

"I am afraid asking would not have helped me much," Justin said, with a smile.

"Well, Nathan do say that they be terrible ignorant folk up there, an' don't know nothing; an' if that be so, I don't s'pose tess much use axin'."

"Well, you know, Amos, it isn't possible for people to know everything."

"No, I spose not. Nathan do say that it's a pity people have to live in them ignorant places. I do wish our Dan'l would git out of it."

"And haven't you heard from him lately?"

"Oah, no. It's months agone now. He said then as 'ow he was workin' on the parish roads under the Corporation. I'm sorry he's workin' under anything. I always think it's healthier, Maister Justin, to work up in the open air."

And Amos, who was a conscientious man, thinking he had wasted quite enough time, turned again to his work.

Mr. Bice did not show his face that day, nor,

indeed, for several days after.   He knew, of
course, that Justin had come home from London,
and concluded that his father had sent for him.
On the whole he was sorry, for Justin was made
of much less pliable material than his father, and
he was anxious to settle the little matter he had
in hand with the least possible amount of
friction ; and, indeed, he had assured his master
that the thing would be done so quietly that no
one would know anything about it until it was
an accomplished fact.   A week before he had felt
certain that he had accomplished his object.   He
had placed before John Pentyre as delicately as
he could the alternative.   His lease of the farm
might be renewed for fourteen years at the same
rental if——

What that "if" was he allowed John to infer.
To his great satisfaction John appeared inclined
to swallow the bait.   Now, however, Justin had
come upon the scene, and that might mean
further arguments and much more drastic
measures.

He knew nothing about Justin personally,
but he had been told that he was a young fellow
of strong will and of unyielding obstinacy, and
it was very likely he would incite his father to
resist even when it could be shown that
resistance was useless.

Mr. Bice was not a man who was much

troubled with scruples. He had one aim in life —to serve his master well; for by serving him he indirectly served himself. Lord Tregeagle, like more than one of his ancestors, had set his heart on painting the map of St. Iago all one colour. The sight of this map, with little dabs of other colour paints, made him irritable, as it had made his father and grandfather irritable before him. Those small freeholders were inter-lopers and intruders, whose presence was offensive, and who were to be got rid of as quickly as possible.

By various methods, known only to the great, and rich, and strong, most of them had been got rid of. John Pentyre was the last of any conse-quence that remained, and how he was to be removed was for a long time a puzzle.

Mr. Bice, however, had staked his reputation on the accomplishment of the task, and for many years had been exercising his wits in all direc-tions. At last, however, by various little tricks and manœuvres, he had fully convinced himself that if John Pentyre had ever possessed the deeds of Endilloe he had lost them.

Having come to that conclusion, he fancied that he would be quite safe in playing a game of bluff, and up to now the results had been quite satisfactory. John Pentyre had fallen into the trap in the most simple and head-over-heels fashion.

"We are quite safe, my lord," Mr. Bice said to his master one evening. "Pentyre rode into Trelford yesterday to consult his lawyer, and to-day, by Jove! he's as meek as Moses."

"Is that so?"

"I assure you he's quite a different man. A few days ago he stood on his dignity and nearly ordered me off the premises. To-day all the fight has gone out of him. Hence, the thing is as plain as a pikestaff. He believed that Nankivel had the deeds, and discovered that he hadn't, and so he sees that he may as well give in quietly."

"Of course," answered Lord Tregeagle. "It's absurd, on the face of it, to suppose that he had any real title to the place. It's hardly likely that the farm would be ours without the house and tenements."

"That's quite true, my lord; so we'll colour that part of the map red without further delay."

Nevertheless, Mr. Bice was by no means pleased when he heard that John Pentyre's son had come home. At first he hoped that it was only for a brief visit, and that in a few days he would be off again, in which case he would keep away from Endilloe until he had taken his departure. Before a week was over he discovered that Justin had come home for good.

"H'm," he reflected, rubbing his chin between

his forefinger and thumb; "I shall have to face it out with both of them. Well, it can't be helped, and the sooner it is over the better."

So on the following morning he made straight for Endilloe, walked boldly up the garden to the front door and gave a loud knock.

CHAPTER XIX

AN INTERVIEW

" He is a hard man who is only just,
And he a sad man who is only wise."

JUSTIN was sole occupant of the " best kitchen "
when Mr. Bice was shown in. Dorothy closed
the door on the steward, and retreated. Mr.
Bice coughed, and looked uncomfortable.

" It was your father I particularly wished
to see this morning," he said.

" He is out on the farm somewhere," Justin
answered. " I have no doubt my sister will
tell him that you are here. Will you not sit
down ? "

" Thank you, I will. I have had a longish
walk this morning, and the weather is getting
quite warm."

" You have come to see my father about the
farm, I presume ? " Justin said, ignoring the
weather question entirely.

" Well, yes. You see, Midsummer will be

upon us directly; and you are aware, perhaps, that his lease expires at that time."

"I believe he has asked for the renewal of it more than once?"

"Well, yes; that is so. But such a request always involves several things. The farm is worth considerably more than it was fourteen years ago, hence a readjustment of rent is necessary."

"You would charge my father for his own improvements?"

"I do not look at the question in that way. The value of a farm may be increased in many ways. There may be an increased demand for farm produce, through some new town springing up in the neighbourhood, or a new railway may give increased facilities for transport——"

"Neither of which has happened in this district," Justin interrupted.

"Exactly. I was simply showing how land values vary from time to time, and that consequently rents had to be readjusted."

"But when the increased value is entirely owing to the farmer's own labour, what then?"

"That, of course, depends on circumstances. If the farmer has had a long lease, and has reaped the full benefit of his improvements, no injustice is done when his rent is raised."

"But who decides that question?"

"I decide it, of course."

"Oh, indeed! Then I presume you intend to raise my father's rent?"

"That does not necessarily follow. I intend to raise the rent of the farm. Indeed, a dozen people will give thirty pounds a year more than your father is giving for it."

"For the farm alone?"

"For the farm, orchard, and tenements—the whole thing complete."

"No doubt they would; but, seeing that the orchard and tenements are not part of the concern, it is not worth while discussing it."

"You think so—eh?"

"I am quite sure of it."

"You are young yet, and I presume your father has not taken you into his confidence."

"You are presuming considerably too much," Justin answered, nettled more at the tone than at the words of his visitor; "I have my father's fullest confidence in everything."

"Indeed! Then he will have told you of our conversations?"

"He has."

"And of certain conditions I hinted at on which the lease of the farm might be renewed?"

"I believe you made no definite promise on that point?"

"Perhaps not; but I gave a pretty broad hint."

"That may be; but hints would hardly be considered evidence in a court of law."

"We are not talking about law courts. But why does not your father come in? He must know I am here waiting for him."

"My father has left all the arrangements with me. But he will be coming in directly, you may be quite sure."

"Then I would prefer to wait for him."

"As you will. But I can assure you that he will do nothing that I do not approve of."

"Then he is a fool, that's all I've got to say."

"It would be much less cowardly if you were to say that to his face. But, in any case, I warn you not to repeat it;" and a light came into Justin's eyes Mr. Bice did not at all appreciate.

For a moment or two there was an awkward silence; then the steward began again.

"The sooner this matter is settled the better it will be for all concerned," he said; "and the less feeling there is imported into it the better it will be for your father in particular."

"Then you should not begin by calling names," Justin said.

"And you should not end, young man, by

being impertinent. But let that pass. Your father wants a renewal of his lease?"

"That is so."

"Then I am prepared to state in black and white that he can have another fourteen years' lease without increase of rent, but on one condition."

"And what is that?"

"That he relinquishes once and for all any foolish claim he professes to have on any portion of the Endilloe estate. This I consider is a very generous offer, and your father will be a very foolish man if he does not close with it."

"But why should he relinquish his own at your suggestion?" Justin asked, quietly.

"It is not his own. He has neither claim nor title to the place."

"Then how did he get it?"

"Oh, that is easy enough of explanation. Originally the whole parish of St. Iago belonged to the Tregeagles. But Roger, the fifth Earl, was a wastrel. He simply let things slide; borrowed money of his tenants, and when they recouped themselves by keeping back the rent he let them. So, having started on the business of not paying rent, a lot of them found it so much to their liking that they never took up the practice again. In time they laid claim to their farms, pretending that they had bought them, and that they had all the necessary papers, and all that kind of thing, and so the claim was allowed to go by default."

"Indeed. So an early ancestor of ours stole Endilloe from Lord Tregeagle?"

"Not a doubt of it."

"And who did Tregeagle steal it from originally?"

"Oh, this is merely wasting words," Mr. Bice said, impatiently.

"Very good," said Justin, colouring slightly. "And in order to avoid any further waste, either of words or time, let me say at once, that whatever becomes of my father's application for a renewal of the lease, neither of us would ever think of giving up our claim to Endilloe."

"But why talk of claim? Where are your deeds? Show your title to the place, and then we will talk about claim."

"Will you show us Lord Tregeagle's title to Endilloe Farm, which was for so long a time in the possession of the Pentyres?"

"Lord Tregeagle's title is not in dispute," said Mr. Bice, shortly.

"But I say it is in dispute," said Justin, hotly. "I have disputed it ever since I was old enough to think about the matter at all."

Mr. Bice laughed. Justin's contention appeared to him in the light of a good joke.

"Then I understand you refuse to come to terms?" he said at length.

"We refuse to come to such terms as you have named, at any rate.

"Then understand that you will leave Endilloe at Midsummer.

"I can assure you," Justin said, with a smile, "that we have no intention of doing anything of the sort."

"Then Lord Tregeagle will find means of evicting you. For generations you have been occupying, rent free, premises that do not belong to you. At Midsummer that state of things will end."

"Indeed. How does Lord Tregeagle propose getting us out?"

"There will be no difficulty in that. The arm of the law is quite strong enough to accomplish much more difficult tasks."

"The law, I believe, respects legal documents," Justin said, quietly.

"But where are your legal documents?" Mr. Bice said, colouring and starting to his feet. "Why don't you show your bogus deeds, if you have them?"

"That's our concern," Justin answered, in a tone of scorn. "But you may be quite sure we shall enforce our claim at the proper time."

Mr. Bice appeared quite taken aback, and after a moment or two he sat down again.

"Look here," he said. "You may as well act sensibly in this matter. If you have any kind of legal claim whatever to the place, of course that claim will be considered and respected. But Lord Tregeagle is convinced that you have no title, and, consequently, he is determined to be no longer kept out of his own."

"No one has any wish to deprive Lord Tregeagle of his rights," was the reply, "and equally we have no desire that we should be deprived of our rights by Lord Tregeagle."

At that moment John Pentyre came into the room with the air of a man who was to be burnt at the stake, but who was determined to put the best face on the matter possible. Mr. Bice turned to him at once.

"Your son tells me," he said, in his most rasping tones, "that you refuse to renew the lease on the conditions I laid down."

"Yes, I believe that is so," John answered mildly.

"You believe it is so? Then you are not sure?"

"Well, yes; I may say we are sure."

"Well, then, why did you not say so at once?" he snapped.

"Because I chose to answer questions in my own way," John said, doggedly.

Mr. Bice looked at him in surprise. This mild-spoken man would evidently show fight if provoked.

"Then what do you propose to do?" he asked at length.

"To stay where we are," John replied.

"But I shall let the farm to somebody else."

"Well, there's nothing to hinder you that I know of."

"But whoever takes the farm will take the house and outbuildings along with it."

"Oh, will he? Not while I'm here, he won't."

Mr. Bice rose and walked towards the door. "Of course," he said, pausing and facing round again, "if you like to push the matter to extremes, you must pay the penalty of your foolishness. You can hardly think it likely that Lord Tregeagle will be defied or worsted by a man like you."

"I expect Lord Tregeagle will have to respect the law like other folk," John answered, quietly.

Mr. Bice snorted. He was a lawyer, and prided himself on his legal knowledge.

"Look here, my friend," he said, patronizingly, "when a case gets into the law courts,

P

you take my word for it, it's the longest purse that wins."

"But law is justice," said John, innocently.

Mr. Bice snorted again. "It is evident you have not had much experience of the law courts," he said. "Law is a machine for squeezing money out of both parties, and the one that can hold out longest wins."

"Then the law is a fraud," John said, angrily.

"Well, my friend, in the main it is," was the cynical answer. "But it is a wonderful institution, nevertheless. It keeps tens of thousands of us in comfortable berths, and it provides a vast fund of entertainment for others who are willing to pay the piper."

"But the laws are made by Parliament," John said, aghast.

"Exactly," was the reply. "And Parliament is composed mainly of lawyers and landowners, who naturally look after their own interests. They make a show of mending the Constitution every now and then, which, of course, makes more work for the lawyers. So if you take my advice—and as a lawyer I am going against my own interests—don't have anything to do with the law. Your little house and tenements here would be swallowed up in a week in lawyers' fees. I have made you a good offer— a very generous offer. It is as your friend I

"THEN THE LAW IS A FRAUD!"

make it. In a fight with Lord Tregeagle you are bound to lose. Think over it again, and come and see me at my office to-morrow." And without waiting for a reply, he walked out of the room.

John and Justin looked at each other for a moment in silence. The older man was the first to speak.

"You see, my son, he speaks fair," he said.

"So does the devil!" was the abrupt reply.

"But there's reason in what he says, too."

"And policy," was the answer."

"But we're bound to lose."

"Well, better lose in the right than succeed in the wrong."

"As you will. If we had only the papers, I would not mind; but everything seems to be against us."

"Even the papers may be discovered yet, and, if not, he will hesitate to take extreme measures."

"Why?"

"Because he is by no means sure that we have not all the necessary documents wherewith to establish our claim."

"But he has a pretty shrewd guess."

"But guesses are not evidence. I bluffed the old skinflint to pretty good tune before you came in. When he arrived he was fully convinced that we had no documents at all. He is by no means certain of it now."

But this style of argument gave John very little comfort. He had not come of a fighting race, or the Endilloe estate would not have dwindled to such meagre proportions. His mind was constantly harassed with doubt as to whether discretion would not be the better part of valour.

He could have another lease of fourteen years on the old terms, and for that period Endilloe would be as truly his as though he had the deeds locked away in a safe. At the end of fourteen years nothing would matter very much, as far as he was concerned. If he were alive at the time, he would be an old man and past work. Hence, under all the circumstances, he was by no means sure that resistance was of the least possible use.

He kept his thoughts to himself, however. He had brought Justin back from London, and had promised to stand by him in the fight. But the more he thought about the matter, the more he was convinced that theirs was a lost cause, and that the battle was bound to end in disaster.

CHAPTER XX

AN ULTIMATUM

" 'Tis a bold game to play,
    Yet I must risk it."

AFTER the visit of Mr. Bice there was a period of calm, extending over several weeks. Justin, who fully believed that the deeds of the estate were in existence somewhere, searched high and low for the missing documents, and hoped almost against hope that before quarter-day came he would be able to flourish them in the face of Lord Tregeagle's steward.

In the numerous closets and cupboards and presses of the old house, letters and papers had accumulated for a hundred and fifty years, and to go through each bundle carefully not only required time but an infinite amount of patience. During the first week Justin did little or nothing else. Then came an offer from Captain Tom Bassett, who, with his two brothers, Richard and Manuel, owned Treskiddy Mine on the other side of the valley. This offer was too good to be lightly thrown aside. The Bassett brothers were working miners. They knew all about "lodes," and "drifts," and "cross-cuts," and "faults." They knew also how to extract the tin from the ore, and were authorities on "strips," and "wracks," and "buddles." But the commercial side of the business they knew practically nothing about. Book-keeping was a science they had never mastered, and the usages of the commercial world occasioned them considerable uneasiness.

They had started several years previously to work Treskiddy as a private venture, and being frugal and industrious men and the price of tin also taking a turn for the better, they managed to make a little money. This they spent in further developing their property till, by-and-by, they became men of some importance in the parish of St. Iago.

But the old habit of doing everything themselves clung to them; while the idea of having a stranger to keep their accounts was most repugnant to them. So Manuel superintended affairs underground, Richard was "Cap'n" on the "floors," and Tom, being the eldest, did the buying and selling, and was, in fact, general manager.

Of late, however, Captain Tom had felt that he was getting entirely out of his depth. The business of the mine had increased very considerably; the number of men, women, and boys employed was larger than ever before; and the wage-sheet had grown to very considerable dimensions. Captain Tom did his best to keep his books in proper order; but, in spite of all his efforts, backed up as they were by the assistance of his brothers, his accounts got beyond him. So perplexed was he at times that he did not know on which side the balance was, or indeed if there was any balance at all.

Moreover, in making contracts for timber, and tools, and machinery, and powder and fuse, and the general stores of a mine, he felt that he was at a disadvantage. His excursions into arithmetic had never advanced beyond a simple rule-of-three sum. Hence, when prices ran off into decimals, and sellers talked about point this and that, and gave him quotations in the unfamiliar jargon of the Stock Exchange, and enlarged on the subject of discounts and the Bank-rate, and other matters that Captain Tom knew nothing about, he felt, in a vague way, that he was at their mercy, and that they could cheat him right and left, without his knowing anything about it.

Evening after evening the brothers sat with their heads together trying to straighten things out.

Prosperity had its drawbacks as well as its advantages. They had become people of considerable importance in the parish, and as large employers of labour—that is, large for St. Iago— were looked up to and consulted in all local affairs; but the responsibilities more than outweighed the honours. They were really happier in the old days than now.

Justin arrived home when Captain Tom's perplexity had reached an acute stage. For several evenings the brothers had discussed the advisability of bringing in an outsider to assist in the management of the commercial side of their business. But who could they get? It was no joke letting a stranger into their secrets. He might land them in worse difficulties than those from which they were now trying to escape.

"How would young Pentyre do?" suggested Manuel, slowly and diffidently, as they sat together one evening in earnest confabulation.

The others looked up with a questioning expression in their eyes, but did not venture any reply.

"He's honest, at any rate," went on Manuel, feeling as though he had been thrown upon the defensive, "and we've known him ever since he was a boy."

"Ay, that's true enough," assented Richard.

"And he's had a good deal of experience,"

continued Manuel. "He practically managed them stores down at Trelford, and since then he's been to London, and in a very important situation too, they do say."

"Richard and Tom looked at their brother with great interest, and waited for him to enlarge upon the theme; but Manuel had exhausted all his stock of arguments, and was perforce reduced to silence.

Captain Tom sighed at length, and remarked that they might do worse.

Manuel's face brightened. "What do you think of it, Richard?" he questioned.

"I agree with Tom," was the reply.

The ice was now fairly broken, and for the next hour Justin's merits and demerits were discussed with much animation.

On the following morning Captain Tom came across to Endilloe, and with much diffidence and circumlocution, broached the subject to Justin, explaining, at the same time, with considerable candour, the reasons for the innovation.

Had Justin been offered the post of Home Secretary he could scarcely have been more surprised.

"It will require time to think about," he said. "If you will give me a few days, I will let you know."

Captain Tom was manifestly disappointed.

The possibility of Justin declining the offer had never once occurred to either of the brothers. "If you think the salary is too small," he said, with energy, "I'll spring another five pound; there now."

"It is not a question of salary at all," Justin answered, with a smile. "I must know first what I am undertaking."

"But you know all 'bout buying and selling?" persisted Captain Tom.

"I understand some markets fairly well," Justin said, evasively.

"And you be good at figures?"

"Fairly good."

"And you know what book-keeping is?"

"Yes."

"Then you are just the man for the job. Say yes and have done with it."

"Let me walk across with you to the mine and go more fully into the matter," Justin persisted. "It would be foolish for me to undertake what I cannot possibly perform."

"Oh, you can do it right enough," Captain Tom said, impatiently. "It's as easy as winkin' to a man who understands figures."

Nevertheless Justin spent two whole days at Treskiddy, and then announced that he would undertake the position and do his best.

Dorothy was delighted, while John regarded

it as a direct interposition of Providence. For
the next two or three weeks the search for
lost documents at home was left entirely in
the hands of Dorothy, but without success.
Dorothy's hope had lain in a strong oaken chest,
built into the wall and so forming a window-seat
at the top of the stairs. This chest had evidently
been intended as a receptacle for valuable
documents. Its corners were clamped with
brass, while the lock was strong enough for a
church door.

Dorothy spent hours kneeling before this
chest, for it was full to the brim of papers of all
sorts. Some of the documents were so interesting that she forgot all about the object of her
search. Letters written by hands long since
mouldered into dust carried her back in imagination to a time when the Pentyres were
people of considerable importance in the county.

On the left-hand side was a set of drawers
occupying the entire width of the box from top
to bottom. Some of these drawers were full
of love-letters carefully tied with ribbon.

Dorothy read a few of them; she could not
help it. Besides, all the people were dead and
forgotten, so what did it matter? But some of
those old love-letters stirred her heart very
strangely. They might have been written only
yesterday. The world had doubtless changed

a good deal in a hundred years, but the human heart remained the same. How easy it would be to construct a romance out of those old letters. Those early Pentyres loved, and hoped, and despaired, as she had done. And then she fell to thinking of Tom Pendarvis, and the letters faded from her sight and time passed away unheeded. What an age it seemed since he went away, and no single word had come to break the long silence. Had he forgotten her? Had he failed in the struggle of life? Was all her love wasted? Would he never come back to her again?

She drew a long sigh after awhile, and said to herself that it didn't matter; that in a few years she would have gone the way of the other Pentyres; that in the grave there was neither love nor regret; that in the coming years her love-story would be no more to any one than the love-stories contained in those faded letters.

All of which might be quite true. But such philosophizing brought her no satisfaction. Tom Pendarvis was everything to her now, and the assurance of his love was of more importance than everything else on earth.

But in spite of day-dreams the search went steadily on. When Justin had got the affairs of the Bassett brothers into something like shape, he was able to join Dorothy again in the quest. But nothing came of it, and quarter-day was drawing perilously near.

Bice, meanwhile, was keeping quiet and playing a waiting game. He did not know how much was behind Justin's game of bluff, and was sometimes inclined to think that their position was much more secure than he had imagined. He was afraid to play a bold game lest in the end all his cards should be trumped; that was the one contingency he dreaded. If the Pentyres got the upper hand of him he would be the laughing-stock of the whole district. He knew that nobody loved him, and that there wasn't a man in the parish of St. Iago who wouldn't rejoice to see him worsted in a game of wits.

As quarter-day drew near Justin grew desperate, and at length, from a strategic point of view, did an exceedingly foolish thing. Instead of going to the mine one morning he walked to Trelford, and was soon closeted with Lawyer Nankivel.

The old lawyer listened to Justin's story with quiet interest, and when it was ended said, in quite a matter-of-fact sort of way—

"Are you quite certain that the deeds you have been searching for ever existed?"

Justin started and then his face fell. "No,"

he said, slowly, "I have no absolute proof. As a matter of fact, we have always taken it for granted."

"You should take nothing for granted," the old lawyer said, sententiously.

"But in such a case we had a right to," Justin answered, with spirit. "Endilloe has been in the possession of the Pentyres for generations. There must have been a title to the property originally."

"That by no means follows. People got property in curious ways in olden times. Tregeagle himself would have a difficulty in showing title for half of his possessions."

"But he manages to keep them."

"Exactly. No one disputes his right or shows a better claim."

"And it's a foul shame that he should dispute our right," Justin said, bitterly. "Because he is a lord, and rich, he can play the tyrant or the rogue with impunity."

The lawyer smiled but did not reply. Justin bit his lip, and for a few moments was silent, then he said—

"Are you sure that you have not the deeds in any of your numerous safes and boxes?"

"Quite sure."

"Have you ever looked for them?"

"No, I have not. There has been no necessity."

"Will you make a search? This is a matter of considerable importance to us."

"If you particularly wish it, yes. But you can hardly expect me to waste my time and the time of my clerks for nothing."

"I expect nothing of the kind," Justin said, sharply. "I expect your accounts have always been settled when they have been sent in."

"Of course they have. I did not mean to suggest anything of the kind."

Justin went back to his work feeling anything but hopeful, but he anticipated no immediate trouble.

How Mr. Bice got to know what transpired in the lawyer's office is not for any one to say. Suffice it, he did get to know, and he rubbed his hands with great glee.

"Now I'm absolutely certain," he said to himself. "The young fool has played into my hands beautifully."

Mr. Nankivel concluded his search on June 19th, and sent word at once that the deeds were not in his possession. On June 20th Mr. Bice sent in his ultimatum. It was short and to the point. If they were not out of the house by the 25th they were to take the consequences of the law. Moreover, if they offered any resistance, summary measures would be adopted. Also claim would be made for arrears of rent in respect of the last ten years that John Pentyre had occupied Endilloe—years during which Lord Tregeagle had waived his claim.

"But he never demanded rent for the house," John said, staring at the notice.

"Are you sure?" Justin questioned.

John's face fell. "I did pay him half a crown for something about ten years ago, but it couldn't have been called rent."

Justin was silent. He feared that such payment might be regarded in law as a recognition of Lord Tregeagle's claim, in which case he would have the right to evict.

CHAPTER XXI

A STRANGER

"We will not from the helm to sit and weep ;
But keep our course, though the rough winds say no."

JOHN PENTYRE read Mr. Bice's letter in absolute silence. He would not blame anybody, not even himself. He had done the best he knew, and if he had made a mistake he would bear the consequences without whining. Justin and Dorothy went out into the orchard, and talked the matter over in the shadow of the trees. Mrs. Pentyre retired to her bedroom, and eased her heart in a flood of tears.

"What shall we do, Justin?" Dorothy said, with a little catch in her breath.

"Stay where we are," he replied.

"Hadn't we better go out quietly?"

"No ; let him put us out by force. It will be an object-lesson to the parish."

"I am afraid it won't do the parish any good."

"Perhaps not. The people have become such serfs that they scarcely any longer resent the brutal rule of wealth and monopoly. Still, we should be cowards if we yielded tamely."

"Do you think he will resort to extreme measures?" Dorothy asked, timidly.

"I've not a doubt of it. He would enjoy nothing better than battering the house down about our ears."

"And will you let him do it?"

"If he likes. You and mother can go to some safe place, and father and I will keep the castle."

Dorothy's eyes sparkled. "Nay," she said, "I will stay and see the fun."

John Pentyre, however, had no idea of any such resistance. On the following morning, without telling any one of his intentions, he made his way by the shortest cuts to the steward's house.

Mr. Bice was at breakfast, and was in no humour to hurry over his meal. John sat on the edge of a chair, in a shabby little room, and twirled his hat between his hands. A cheap Swiss clock ticked loudly on the mantelpiece. Every now and then John glanced up to see how the time was progressing, and sighed as he did so. Surely fingers never moved so slowly on a dial before.

Mr. Bice stalked in at length without ceremony, picking his teeth with a quill.

"Oh, good morning!" he said, abruptly, as though he had not the remotest idea who was waiting for him.

"Good morning," John said, nervously. "I've come to see you about that notice you sent last evening."

"Plain enough, wasn't it?"

"Yes; it was plain enough. I want you to take it back.

"You do—eh?" and Mr. Bice smiled good-humouredly. "Don't like the prospect—eh?" and his smile became broader. "Own yourself beaten—eh?" and he laughed outright.

"I have been unable to find the deeds," John said, plaintively.

Mr. Bice's face changed in a moment. "You never expected to find them," he said, angrily. "People can't find things that have no existence."

"But they existed once," John said, humbly.

"You try to think so, no doubt. But the truth is you and your rascally ancestors have been living for generations on stolen property."

"You are safe, no doubt, in abusing dead people," John answered, with a quick flash in his eye; "they are unable to defend themselves."

Mr. Bice winced, and set his teeth tightly together.

"For myself," John went on, "I have always believed that the title was good. Unfortunately, however, I cannot produce it. For that matter, you cannot produce any title to it, either."

"But we can," snapped Mr. Bice.

"Then it is a bogus one," John said, with spirit, "and I am too weak to contest it. In cases of this kind, it is the strong who win. I've come to recognize the inevitable, or I shouldn't have come here this morning."

"Well, and what do you want?" growled the steward.

"I want to keep the farm; and, for the sake of it, I'll give up Endilloe."

"No doubt of it. I thought you would come to your senses some time. It's a pity you've been so long over it."

"I've tried to do what is right," John said, humbly.

"You have, eh? Then all I can say is that your notions of right are somewhat peculiar;" and Mr. Bice chuckled.

John flushed, but did not speak. Mr. Bice walked to the window and made more ostentatious use of his toothpick. On the whole he was enjoying the interview. To see John

Pentyre humble and at his feet was like nectar to him.

"You hardly expect me, of course," he said at length, "to offer you the old terms?"

"Why not?" John questioned, timidly.

"Why not? Well, the reasons are too numerous to mention. I've proved my case since then. The element of doubt has disappeared. You own yourself that you occupy property that you have no right to."

"I own to nothing of the kind," John said, hotly.

"What?" and Mr. Bice faced round with a blaze of passion in his eyes.

"I've every moral right to the place," John continued. "I've the right of long possession. But Endilloe is of very little use to me without the farm. You know that. That's where you've got the upper hand of me."

"And what is more, we intend to keep it," was the reply. "You have been defiant, sir, and even impudent, now you will take the consequences."

"You mean——"

"I mean exactly what I said in my letter yesterday. I am not in the habit of changing my mind two or three times a day. Now go home and get ready to quit, for if you are in the place an hour beyond the time, by Heaven you'll rue it!"

"And this is your final answer?"

"It is."

"Then you'll rue it also;" and John rose suddenly to his feet and made for the door. His gentle eyes were blazing, his lips were white with anger. Mr. Bice had supplied him with the fillip he needed. By the time he reached Endilloe he was more eager than Justin to fight the battle to the death.

In one of the nearer fields he stumbled across Nathan and told him how matters stood.

"And be you agoin' to stick out?" Nathan asked.

"To the last gasp," was the reply.

"Then I'm yer man," said Nathan. "Endilloe ain't got three-foot walls and oaken doors for nothin'. My stars, we'll have a time of it."

"You'll stand by me, Nathan?"

"To the laast, master."

John grasped his hind's hard hand and walked on in silence.

That evening John discussed with Justin and Dorothy plans for defence. His good spirits had quite returned. Indeed, he was the most cheerful of the family.

"We'll have some fun out of the business, at any rate," he said. "And if they get Endilloe won't be worth much to them."

"But we shall have to leave the dear old place in the end," Dorothy said, plaintively.

"I won't even say that," John answered. "There's no knowing what will happen."

During the next day or two John and Justin made preparations for a lengthened siege. They knew the temper of Mr. Bice, and Lord Tregeagle was as reckless as his steward when his blood was up. Mr. Bice was careful to omit no legal formality, and in every case acted on the assumption that Lord Tregeagle's claim was indisputable.

John sent him word that he disputed Lord Tregeagle's claim, and that he should defend his home if needs be with his life. That any person seen about the place would be regarded as a trespasser and would be treated accordingly. That Endilloe was well furnished with fire-arms and other means of defence, that he and his family had counted the costs and were prepared to abide by the consequences.

Mr. Bice read John's letter with knitted brows and a troubled light in his eyes. He had made a mistake in estimating his character. He had expected a flash of temper now and then, but he had not anticipated any real resistance. He was sorry now that he had not accepted John's offer. To evict people by force was always an unpleasant task; besides, it would rouse the slumbering antagonism of every man in the parish.

But he had gone too far to draw back. He would have to carry the matter through whatever the consequences might be. To own himself defeated would make him the laughing-stock of the whole district and set every other small freeholder at defiance; so he sent him word that he would give him till six o'clock on Thursday evening to clear out in a quiet and orderly fashion. If, however, he was not out of the house, bag and baggage, by that time, a sufficient force of police would be on hand to evict him in a manner that might not be altogether pleasant.

To this John sent no reply, and so matters remained until the fateful day.

On the evening previous John and his two children were discussing events, as they had discussed them a hundred times before. They talked quietly and without passion, while the twilight of the long summer day deepened rapidly. Every now and then a long pause intervened, for each had thoughts which even the nearest of kin might not share. Dorothy thought of Tom Pendarvis, and wondered why he kept silent so long. Justin thought of Ruby; he could not help it. She might be the wife of another; but that could not alter the fact that she had stolen his heart, and he honestly believed that he would never love again.

During one of those pauses the door opened, and Mrs. Pentyre came into the room.

"Dorothy," she said, "there is a man at the back door who wants to see you. He does not give his name, but he says he has a message for you."

"Wants to see me?" Dorothy questioned, turning quickly round. "What is he like?"

"Well, I couldn't see his face very plainly, for it's darker out in the porch than here; but he looks quite an elderly man."

Dorothy hesitated, and looked at her brother. "I don't expect he will eat you," Justin said, with a laugh. "You had better go and see what he wants."

"He looks to be very respectably dressed," Mrs. Pentyre interposed.

"I expect he's on some begging expedition," Dorothy said, with a laugh. "However, I will go and interview him."

Mrs. Pentyre took Dorothy's chair, and conversation started afresh.

Dorothy found the stranger sitting on a bench, in the shadow of a large thorn tree, a few paces from the door. He raised his brown wideawake hat as she came towards him, and she saw that his hair, as well as his beard, was quite white. But he made no attempt to rise.

"You are Miss Dorothy Pen—Pentyre?" he questioned, in a low, husky voice, as though he were suffering from a cold.

"Yes," she said; "that is my name. Did you wish to see me?"

"I have a message for Miss Dorothy Pentyre," he answered, slowly, and in the same husky tones; "and I am to deliver it only to her."

"A message from whom?" she questioned, doubtfully.

"From Tom Pendarvis," he answered slowly. "Poor Tom! he never tired of talking about you."

"Then you know him?" she questioned, eagerly.

"I knew him once, miss—knew him well."

"But where and when?"

"In the Transvaal, miss. We were comrades, and, as a rule, we cared for no other company."

"And did he get on?" she asked, eagerly— "that is, did he work hard, and try his best?"

"He did, miss; he worked almost night and day. He was always something of a schemer, so he told me, and he invented a machine for boring rock and another for crushing ore; but it nearly killed him. It isn't safe to burn the candle at both ends, miss."

"Oh, I knew he would get on, if he had the chance!" she said, clasping her hands tightly together. "But why did he not send word? Why did he not let me know?"

"People do not get on in a day," was the answer. "And then he fell ill; and when he lay at the point of death, I promised him I'd come and see you, if I ever visited the Old Country again, and tell you that he never wavered in his love for you—no, not for a moment."

"Then—then—he's—he's—dead?" she gasped, leaning against the porch for support.

"No; don't say that, miss—don't say that! There was still life in him when I left the Transvaal; and if I could only send him word that you loved him still, I believe it would do him more good than all the medicine in the world."

"Oh, how could he ever doubt me!" she wailed.

"He thought you were like the rest, miss—that you had lost faith in him."

"But I never did lose faith in him—never, never!" she cried. "He only wanted an opportunity. He was cleverer than all his companions put together."

"Then your message is reconciliation?" he said.

"'Reconciliation?'" she cried. "Oh no; that is not the right word! We never quarrelled. Tom was proud; he thought I was dissatisfied, and so he went away. Tell him I have never changed."

"I will, miss."

"And tell him—oh, tell him!—that I want him to come home. He will understand that."

"He will be very stupid if he don't, miss."

"But letters are so slow. Could you not telegraph to him? Oh, if he only knew, I am sure he would not stay away!"

"Let me think, miss;" and the old man leant his elbows upon his knees, and buried his face in his hands. And when he raised his head again the wideawake hat lay on the ground, and a young man sat in his place under the tree.

CHAPTER XXII

THE EVE OF THE BATTLE

> "Love has so filled my heart,
> That there is no room for fear."

DOROTHY darted forward with a glad cry: "Oh, Tom, Tom!" and the next moment they were clasped in each other's arms. For awhile a sweet rain of kisses put an end to speech. Then Dorothy drew herself away and said: "But how could you, Tom?"

"I couldn't resist the temptation, darling," he said, with a laugh. "I had read about it being done in novels, and I thought I would like to make the experiment, though, candidly, I did not think it would succeed."

"And it wouldn't have succeeded, only it was so nearly dark."

"Exactly; that was part of the little scheme."

"And did you really think, you naughty boy, that I had changed?"

"I did not know what to think, Dorothy. A lot may happen in three or four years."

"But it's a poor love that won't endure a much longer silence than that."

Yes, I know. But I feared you would think I was an utter failure, and so put me out of your thoughts. Such things have happened, you know. And sometimes new loves have driven out the old."

"And if I had changed, Tom?"

"Then I should have gone away quietly, and no one would have known that I had been. That was my little plot, Dorothy."

"And you are glad that you had to reveal yourself?"

And for answer he kissed her again and again.

Two or three minutes later Justin came upon the scene, much wondering what had become of his sister. Dorothy was telling Tom of the notice they had to quit, and what preparations they were making in face of siege; and so interested were they both, that they did not hear the door open, and were unconscious of the fact that Justin stood in the porch staring at them.

As a matter of fact, Justin was too astonished to speak. It had grown too dark for him to distinguish faces; but Dorothy's voice was unmistakable, nor was it so dark but that he could see she sat close to the stranger, and, what was more, that he had his arm about her waist.

The proper thing to have done would have been to have coughed. He had read novels enough to understand that. In books, properly conducted people always cough when they wish to make their presence known. But Justin was too astonished, not to say indignant, to act in any such considerate fashion. As soon as he recovered himself, he exclaimed in a tone of righteous indignation—

"Dorothy, what is the meaning of this?"

Instantly she was on her feet. "Oh, Justin," she cried, coming towards him with outstretched hands, "Tom has come home?"

"Tom?" he questioned, doubtfully. "You mean Tom Pendarvis?"

"Why, of course! What other Tom could I mean?"

"Exactly; there is no other Tom, is there?" and the next moment the two young men had clasped hands, and were looking into each other's faces.

"I am glad to see you home again, Tom," Justin said, heartily; "I am, upon my soul!"

"But not so glad as I am to be at home?" was the reply.

"But when did you come?"

"I landed this morning at Plymouth."

"Ah! been abroad, have you?"

"I have had three years in Africa."

"And have you come home to stay?"

"I hope so. Do you think your father will see me?"

"I don't know. You have come at a good time."

"I might be of service. Defending one's house against attack is common enough in Africa, and I have had plenty of experience."

"Then you are just the man we want. Old Bice vows that if we don't go out quietly, he will evict us by force; and I believe he will try."

"I hope you will stay and help us," Dorothy interposed at this point. "Oh, I hope you will."

"I will, if your father will let me," was the reply.

"That we can easily find out," Justin said; "Dorothy and I will go and send him to you."

In the hall they met John coming to see what had become of them; so, telling him that he was wanted outside, they went in, and waited the result with as much patience as they could command.

Justin and his mother kept up a desultory conversation, but Dorothy was too excited to talk. Mrs. Pentyre was curious to know who the strange man was that had kept them so long; but the only answer she could get was—

"We have sent father to find out."

The old eight-day clock ticked steadily on, and it had grown so dark that they could not see each other's faces; but no attempt was made to light the lamp. Dorothy pleaded that she loved the darkness of a summer's night, and that it was not so dark but that they could see to talk.

So the minutes sped on, and Dorothy's heart kept beating faster and faster. She knew that her cheeks must be burning bright red, and that her eyes would be unusually brilliant. She would not have the lamp lighted just now on any account. She tried to take part in the intermittent talk between her mother and Justin, but words would not come. She was compelled to be silent even against her will.

At length her quick ear detected a footstep; then the door opened. She thought her heart had stopped. Was her father coming back alone? She placed her hand to her side, and held her breath. That was her father's footstep, and his only. No; there was another. Tom was coming with him. It was all right. Her heart bounded on again, but the colour faded suddenly out of her cheeks. She rose tremblingly and went and lighted the lamp, her ears hum-

R

ming strange music all the while. She felt as light as air. All the darkness and oppression had gone out of her heart. It was nothing to her that they were threatened with eviction. Tom had come home, and had made his peace with her father. It must be so, or he would not be coming with him into the house.

She turned from lighting the lamp, and her eyes met her lover's; they were full of light and love. She did not want him to tell her anything then; she knew all.

Mrs. Pentyre was staring at the new arrival in wondering surprise. This was not the stranger she had seen at the back door. But nobody seemed inclined to offer any further explanations.

"Give the boy welcome, mother," John said, with a curious inflection in his voice. "It's all right."

And Mrs. Pentyre, who had always been fond of the light-hearted young fellow, put her arms round his neck and kissed him.

Tom's eyes ran full of tears in a moment. It was a welcome such as he had never expected, and it made him think how much he had lost in the early death of his own mother.

Justin put an end to the general embarrassment by suggesting that supper should be brought in, and Mrs. Pentyre hurried off into the kitchen, followed by Dorthy.

The three men saw little of bed that night. Tom's quick eye and larger experience saw a dozen things that needed doing if the house was to be safely garrisoned; and when morning broke it presented a strange appearance. All the lower windows had been securely boarded up, while the doors were protected by stout deal planks. Indeed, it was quite evident that the defenders meant business; and the news quickly ran through the neighbourhood that the Pentyres intended to defy Lord Tregeagle and the law.

Tom's great regret was that there was not a garden-hose in the house. There was such a magnificent water-supply that he thought it a pity it could not be brought into use.

"A good dousing of cold water," he said to John, "is better than grape-shot for dispersing a crowd."

But John shook his head. Now that his blood was up, he was strongly disposed to give the attacking party a welcome of a somewhat warmer character.

After breakfast, Tom went in search of Nathan.

"Drive over to Trelford at once," he said, "and fetch back twenty yards of rubber tubing;

also nozzle and rose, and a few yards of copper wire."

"What be 'em for?" Nathan asked.

"Oh, I'm going to manufacture a garden-hose!" was the reply. "It will come in handy also for swilling out the stable and many other things."

Nathan scratched his head for several seconds, then walked slowly away, and a quarter of an hour later was driving rapidly in the direction of Trelford. As the day wore away the excitement at Endilloe became intense. No detachment of troops waiting for the first sound of battle was ever more on the alert. That the conflict in which they were engaged was to all appearances destined to end in disaster did not detract in the least from their determination to carry it through to the bitter end. They could but lose. They were bound to lose in any case, and so they would lose fighting. It would be a satisfaction in after years to remember that they had resisted wrong to the best of their ability; that they had not flung away their birthright as though it were a worthless thing.

In the end they had no doubt they would see their furniture thrown pell-mell into the garden, and would find themselves standing outside the house that had so long sheltered them. Such things went on constantly in the

British Isles—not only in the country, but in the chief cities. But a few weeks before they had read in the newspapers how a dozen families had been evicted in a poor part of London, and how their furniture had been stacked in the streets for days on the stretch, and how the poor people sat watching night after night by their household gods. Such martyrdoms might do good in some far-off and round-about way. It was necessary that light should be let in upon the conscience of England on some social and economic questions, and to do this it was needful that some one should suffer.

As John Pentyre sat brooding over his wrongs and waiting for the attack, he was conscious that a change was slowly taking place within him. He had been a most loyal subject, a strict Conservative, a strong upholder of the Constitution, a devout worshipper of the British aristocracy, an implicit believer in the right of those who had to rule over those who had not. Nor had these beliefs been weakened by anything that his neighbours or even his own ancestors had suffered. That the mining industry was crippled by heavy dues, that the small freeholder had practically disappeared from their midst, that the leaseholders were daily wasting their strength and substance for the enrichment of others, were not matters that had troubled him at all.

But somehow now, when his turn had come to be the pipkin between the iron pots, he seemed to see things in a somewhat different light. He did not appreciate being a modern Naboth; the loss of his vineyard touched him to the quick, and the strength of the giants seemed to be more cruelly used than before.

Justin shared very largely his father's thoughts, but Tom and Dorothy had much pleasanter things to think of. Dorothy moved about like one in a dream. It seemed almost too good to be true that Tom should be home again; and every time they met, her face would light up with a fresh accession of joy.

Busy as they were all kept, Tom and Dorothy managed to snatch a good many moments together when no one else was near. They had so much to talk about, so many plans to discuss, so much lost time to make up, that they were often sublimely unconscious of the fact that there were such people as Lord Tregeagle and his steward in the world. The loss of Endilloe seemed a comparatively small matter to Dorothy now that she had found Tom.

At a quarter to six Nathan came to the back door with the tidings that Mr. Bice and two constables were coming up the road in the direction of Endilloe.

Nathan was at once admitted and the door made fast again. Tom had completed his hose arrangement, and satisfied himself that it was in good working order. There was nothing to be done now but to calmly await the issue.

Mr. and Mrs. Pentyre, Justin and Dorothy, took up positions at the upstairs windows. Tom and Nathan remained downstairs. A few minutes before six Mr. Bice was seen to reach the garden gate, accompanied by the constables, and followed at a considerable distance by a crowd of men, women, and children, who evidently intended to see the fun.

At sight of the barricaded house, Mr. Bice paused, and held a hurried consultation with his companions, while the crowd came perceptibly nearer. Mr. Bice evidently felt that his force was not sufficient, particularly as there were clear manifestations that he had a hostile crowd at his back. Nevertheless, his first duty was clear, and that was to go to the house and demand in the name of the law that John Pentyre and his family quietly and at once vacate it. If they still refused, it would be easy to get together a larger force of constables and accomplish by violent measures what could not be done by peaceful ones.

Mr. Bice looked very white as he opened the garden gate, then, with a policeman on either side of him, he marched boldly and pompously towards the house.

CHAPTER XXIII

THE ATTACK

"How oft the sight of means to do ill deeds
    Makes ill deeds done."

MR. BICE was not long in discovering that the whole of the Pentyre family occupied positions at the upstairs windows. This was reassuring. It implied that the resistance was to be passive rather than active. There was no sign of guns or of any other deadly weapon. Violence on the part of the Pentyres did not appear to be on their programme. Mr. Bice drew a long breath and began to breathe freely. He was not devoid of courage, but he objected, nevertheless, to being shot at from behind a barricade.

Within a few paces of the front door he paused and looked up at John, who sat at the open window directly above his head.

"Then you are determined to resist the law?" he questioned.

"No, I am not," was the quick reply, "but I'm determined to resist you."

263

"But I have brought, as you see, the officers of the law with me."

"I can't help that."

"But you are foolish to hold out. You have been served with legal notice to quit. You haven't a leg to stand on, either in law or equity. If you won't go out quietly, we are bound to put you out by force. I am sorry to have to do it. But the house is let to another tenant, who is waiting to come in."

"You've no right to let what isn't yours," John said, doggedly. "And as for putting us out by force, well, that's a game that two can play at."

"But you know what resisting the law officers means? You won't find Bodmin Gaol a particularly comfortable place to live in."

"I'm prepared to take my chance of it in any case."

"Then you won't open the door?"

"No, I won't;" and John stamped on the floor, which was a signal to those below.

Tom Pendarvis, with the nozzle of his hose in position, was getting impatient for the talk to end. He was afraid that the tubing would burst, so strong was the weight of water behind.

Mr. Bice's mouth fell open at John's last reply, and he appeared for a moment to be in a brown study.

Tom heard the signal overhead, and turned the tap. The torrent of water leaped out swift and straight as a shaft of light. Tom's aim was accurate. Mr. Bice's open mouth was full to overflowing in a moment. With a gasp and a splutter he sprang a full foot from the ground, the swift jet of water following him and smacking him in the eyes, on the cheeks, and rattling on the starch of his immaculate shirt-front. As soon as he could recover his breath, he yelled at the top of his voice, a yell which was caught up by the crowd, and ended in a roar of derisive laughter.

The policemen endeavoured to take action at once, but a stinging torrent of water straight in their faces was not at all conducive to clearness of vision. They tried bravely to shield their faces with their hands, but no chain gun ever delivered its charges with such rapidity or with such effect as this quick-firing hose.

They ran first this way, then that, gasping, sputtering, swearing, the relentless torrent following them, deafening them, blinding them, and reducing their courage to the consistency of their clothes.

The Pentyres at the upstairs windows laughed till the tears ran down their faces. Such a pantomime they had never seen before, their only regret being that it was so soon over.

The crowd, which by this time had grown to considerable dimensions, laughed, and yelled, and clapped their hands, and almost went into hysterics, while the inglorious three beat a hasty retreat towards the garden gate.

"Now, officers, pluck up your courage, and do your duty," cried a wag in the crowd "Shoulder arms and march."

But the policemen were too crestfallen even to retort.

"Let the women bind up their wounds," some one else shouted; "the poor fellows are ready to faint and die;" and the crowd yelled again.

"Look at old Bice's shirt-front," cried a small boy. "Won't his mother beat him!"

So to a running fire of ridicule and derisive laughter they made their way down the lane as fast as their soaked and clinging clothes would let them. At the bottom their horse and trap were waiting for them, and, climbing into the vehicle with most unseemly haste, they were driven swiftly away in the direction of Trelford.

John Pentyre and his family came out into the garden and held a *levée*. But Tom Pendarvis kept resolutely out of sight, and no one in St. Iago Churchtown knew yet that he had returned.

John was greatly touched by the sympathy of his neighbours, and offers of assistance flowed in upon him from every side.

"I shall not need your help to-day, at any rate," he said, with a smile. "They've had enough for one evening, I reckon."

"Ay, but they'll be round early to-morrow morning, you may depend."

"Most likely they will, and we shall be ready for them."

Before sunset Endilloe had resumed its normal quiet, and there was no sign of any further hostilities. The family sat down to its evening meal in peace, and laughed again and again over the events of the afternoon. Tom further enlivened the proceedings by stories of his adventures in Africa; and little by little it leaked out that he had not returned to England a penniless lover, though to what extent Fortune had smiled upon him he kept to himself.

Justin suggested that they should get to bed early, as they would need to be stirring with the lark in the morning.

Nathan was having supper in the kitchen with Amos Blue, who had pressed to be allowed to assist his master in defending his own.

Suddenly Amos started, and turned his head in a listening attitude.

"There's somebody a-prowlin' about at the back, Nathan, or I'm mistook," he said, under his breath.

"Oh, it's the cows down in the paddock that you hear," Nathan said, knowingly.

"No, it ain't no cows, neither," Amos replied, doggedly. "There's people, or my ears be failin'."

Nathan paused in his eating, and listened.

"I b'leeve you be right, Amos," he said, with a look of concern in his eyes; and he stole across to the back stairs and ran nimbly up.

The night was cloudy, and was consequently as dark as a June night could well be. The window of his own bedroom was slightly open. He crept stealthily towards it and listened. In a few moments he was convinced that a determined attack was to be made upon the house, but this time from the rear. Several men were moving quietly and stealthily about like spectres in the dim light. Nathan strained his eyes, and fancied that he saw a big log of wood, which he had no doubt would be used as a ram against the back door.

"Blow 'em, they've choosed their time well," he said to himself. "They think we're oal off our guard, or else that we're in bed asleep. Howsomever, we'll soon let 'em knaw that they're mistook;" and he ran as nimbly down the stairs as he had run up, and was soon knocking at the door of the living-room.

"Come in," was the quick response; and the next moment Nathan stood before them with a very white face.

"What's up, Nathan?" Justin asked, quickly.

"They be at it again," was the reply, "and they're more ov 'em this time."

"No, surely?"

"As sure, sir, as I be a livin' man."

Tom was out of the room like a shot. But it was no easy matter to direct a hose in the dark. Justin followed him, while John seized his double-barrelled gun, which was loaded with peas, and made his way to his own bedroom. He was not long in discovering what was up. It was clear that a simultaneous attack was to be made on the back and front of the house. Through the open window he saw four men creeping round the end of the house, bearing a big log of wood between them. He waited for them to get into position in front of the door. They stood close together, waiting probably for some signal. John was on his knees, with the muzzle of his gun resting on the window-sill. His finger trembled on the trigger. As yet no sound came from the back. He had better take the initiative; he could see the four heads bent towards each other. He pulled the trigger.

There was a flash—a yell as though all the cats in St. Iago had been suddenly let loose, and the four men cleared the garden fence in as many different directions, using language more lurid and profane than had ever been heard in the peaceful neighbourhood of Endilloe before.

John withdrew his weapon and made for one of the back windows. But the report of his gun and the yell that followed it had evidently frightened the besiegers. He was just in time to see a frenzied retreat over the back wall, the pitiless hose drenching them to the skin as they made frantic and futile efforts to clear the fence at a bound.

But the troubles of the besiegers were not at an end even then. On the other side of the fence were some forty or fifty men and lads, who had come together in anticipation of further entertainment. These set upon the flying and drenched policemen and bailiffs, and mauled them out of sheer mischief. If the first retreat of the evictors was ignominious, the second was even more so. They took to their heels in all directions, and suffered many a scratch and bruise by attacking hedges and falling into pits, the dangers of which were not seen in the darkness.

On the following morning Mr. Bice was almost in despair. He might have the law on his side, but he had no power to enforce it. Policemen were few in that part of the country, and they hated the task. Indeed, it seemed only too clear that all their sympathies were with the besieged farmer.

Moreover, they found themselves derided on every hand. Mocking laughter and insulting words greeted them wherever they showed their faces, and there could be no doubt that in any future attempt to evict the farmer they would have to fight their way through a hostile crowd before they reached the house at all.

Mr. Bice discussed the matter with the Chief Constable from every point of view, and it was ultimately decided that the excitement must be allowed to die down before any further steps were taken. It was very humiliating, no doubt; but in the present temper of the parish it was only too evident that any attempt to evict the farmer by force would lead to a very serious breach of the peace, and probably to bloodshed.

Indeed, so little did the constable like the whole business, and so much did he resent being a mere tool to do Lord Tregeagle's dirty work, that he advised Mr. Bice to accept his defeat and let John Pentyre remain at Endilloe on the old terms. But Mr. Bice swore that he would die first.

"Besides," said he, "I have let the house

s

and farm to another tenant at thirty pounds a year more rent, and I'm bound to carry the thing through."

"You can better afford to lose thirty pounds than have the whole neighbourhood against you," was the reply.

But the steward was obdurate. He had never been defeated yet, and he did not intend to be.

"At any rate," said the constable, "you will have to make-believe that you are. For a week at least you will have to lie low. This ferment and excitement will not die down in a day."

"I know that," was the reply; "and in the meantime we can be preparing our plans. There's no denying that we have bungled the thing—bungled it terribly. We must be careful not to make the same mistake again. Another such fiasco would ruin every one of us."

"It might ruin you," was the laconic reply; and then the discussion ended.

Meanwhile, events were taking shape in another direction which were destined to upset all previous conclusions.

CHAPTER XXIV

TOM MAKES A DISCOVERY

"Good lurks in unexpected places,
    Waiting our need."

THE day after "the raid," as Tom called it, gave
promise of being just as tame as the previous
one had been exciting. It was evident as the
morning wore away, that the evictors were
taking a rest. Not a single policeman showed
his face in the neighbourhood, though miners
by the dozen were seen loitering about, hoping
for a continuance of the fun.

John and his two men went out on the
farm — that is, on John's small demesne of
twenty acres which surrounded his house.
Justin took further leave of absence from the
mine, for his employers were in perfect sympathy with him, and told him that he could
remain away as long as it was necessary for
the defence of his home. Tom would have
found time hang heavy on his hands, only that
Dorothy was constantly flitting about, and a

smile from her every now and then quite satisfied him.

So the morning wore away and afternoon came — a sweet, dreamy, delicious afternoon, when all nature seemed to be at rest; when the very trees nodded in the warm June air and the flowers seemed to fall fast asleep.

Tom and Dorothy found themselves seated in the window on the old oaken chest at the top of the stairs.

Dorothy had been telling her lover of the fruitless search they had made for the missing deeds, and how she had come across bundles of love-letters written by dead-and-gone ancestors and hidden away in a series of drawers that stretched across the end of the box. In describing these drawers she excited Tom's curiosity.

" Were they secret drawers ? " he asked.

"Oh no; there is nothing secret about them."

" Have you the key of the box ? "

"Yes; would you like to look inside ? "

" Very much."

" I don't think I shall let you read any of the letters," she said, with a smile.

" I don't think I want to," he answered; "but the old chest is evidently a curiosity."

In a few minutes the lid was thrown back and the lovers were kneeling before it. Tom, with his trained, mechanical eye, took in all the measurements in a moment.

"You are quite right, Dorothy," he said, "there is nothing secret about the drawers;" and he pulled one of them clean out of its socket.

He gave a low whistle as he did so, and then pulled out a second drawer and a third.

"Why do you do that?" Dorothy asked, glancing curiously at him.

"I wanted to see if they were all of the same depth," he answered.

"And are they?"

"I think so."

"Then your curiosity is satisfied?"

"On the contrary, it is aroused."

"Why, Tom?" and she looked eagerly into his eyes.

For answer he took a small slide-rule from his pocket—which a working engineer is rarely without—and began taking measurements.

Dorothy watched him with intense interest and curiosity.

"Well," she asked at length, "what have you discovered?"

"That there are three inches of space behind these drawers unaccounted for," he answered.

"You are certain?"

"Absolutely."

"And what then?"

He shook his head and laughed. "Now you are getting beyond me, Dorothy," he said; "but we must discover, if we can, if there is any means of getting at the back of these drawers."

"You think there may be something there?"

"There may be. It was the custom in olden times, before steel safes were invented, to contrive all kinds of secret drawers and cabinets for the safe keeping of valuables."

"Oh yes, I know; and Justin examined this box very carefully to see if there was any false bottom in it."

"I don't think there is any false bottom," he said; "but there is a false end, and the question now is how to get at it."

For the next hour there was no love-making between them, which was rather remarkable, considering they were left in undisturbed possession of the landing.

Tom tried to put himself in the position of the man who constructed the box.

"He had to contrive a secret drawer behind those other drawers," he said to himself. "How would he do it?"

As a mechanic, he had to admit that there were several ways.

"For instance," he said to himself, "he might

have done it by——" and he leant forward and carefully examined the construction of the drawers; "but he didn't," he added.

So by a process of elimination and examinations he reduced all possible methods to one.

"These drawers come out *en bloc*," he said to Dorothy; "and there is only one way they can come out. You see how they are dove-tailed into the sides. Hence they must be lifted out." And he got on to his feet and made the attempt.

Dorothy's face fell. There was not the least sign of movement.

"I think you must be mistaken, Tom," she said, "they don't move a bit."

"I hardly expected they would," he said, with a smile. "The man who contrived the thing would also contrive a means of keeping it firmly fixed in its place. That is what we have to find out."

"What *you* have to find out," she said, laughingly. "I am sure I have not one particle of ingenuity in my nature."

"There will be a spring or some other contrivance," he said, reflectively. "I must try to put myself in this old joiner's place again."

Dorothy watched him with growing curiosity and admiration. The three long years that he had been away had changed him in nearly every respect. He was not less generous and light-hearted than in the old days, and yet there was a quiet gravity, an evidence of resource, a reserve of strength, a suggestion of dignity, that were altogether new. The youth had become a man.

"There are three or four ways the thing may be done," he said, looking at Dorothy with a smile. "Let's try the most likely first."

She did not reply, but she watched him as he pulled two of the drawers clean out of their sockets.

Then he put his hand into the vacant space, and felt carefully along the side.

"Ah!" he said, with a little gasp, "it's very cleverly done. These old workmen were no bunglers. Now, Dorothy, we are all right;" and in another moment he had slid out the drawers and laid them on the floor."

"But there's nothing behind, Tom," Dorothy said, disappointedly. "You see, there's only that plain solid end of the box."

"Looks like it, doesn't it?" he said, with a smile; "but that's where the ingenuity of the thing comes in. Now for another secret spring, and this false end will come out."

"But are you sure it's a false end?"

"Quite sure, Dorothy; look at the thickness

of the other end.   Besides, listen," and he tapped it with his slide-rule.

"It doesn't sound very solid, certainly," she said.

"I don't want to prise the thing open if it can be avoided," he went on.   "But if we can find no other way, we'll resort to extreme measures."

"I'm sure you'll find out, if you'll do a little more 'considering,'" she said, with a laugh.

"Here we are at last," he said, after a long interval of silence, "but it's a tight fit." A minute later, and the secret recess was revealed.

"O Tom," Dorothy gasped; and she fell on her knees again before the box.   The recess was full of papers; some of them marked by big blotches of sealing-wax, others carefully tied with tape.

"I believe we are on the right track at last, Dorothy," Tom said, excitedly.   "These are evidently legal documents."

"Let me go and call father and Justin," she said, springing to her feet.

"No, no; not yet," he said.   "Let's not buoy them up with hopes that may end in disappointment.   We'll make an examination first."

Dorothy knelt down again, and together they examined the papers one by one, Dorothy's eyes growing wider and wider all the while.

"You can call your father now," Tom said at length, with a strange thrill in his voice. "By Heaven, we'll turn the tables on old Bice this time."

But Dorothy was too impatient to go downstairs.

"Father — Justin," she called quickly and excitedly; and her voice rang along the corridor and down the stairs clear as a bell.

"What is it?" Justin called from below.

"Come quickly," she cried. "Tom has made a discovery.

Justin knew by the excited tone of her voice something out of the common had happened, and he bounded up the stairs three steps at a time.

"What!" he cried, as soon as he reached the top. "Have you found the deeds?"

"Ay! They're all here," Tom said, quietly.

Justin sat down on the floor, looking very white, and looked at the papers one after the other, while Dorothy went off in search of her father.

In the kitchen she came upon her mother, busy as usual.

"Oh, mother," she exclaimed, "we've found the deeds at last."

"No!"

"As true as I'm living, mother. Where's father?"

"He was in the back yard a few minutes ago."

Dorothy was out of the house in a moment. John was standing against a gate with his arm on the top rail, looking wistfully across the smiling landscape. The reaction had already begun to set in. He was fighting a losing battle, playing the part of an obstinate, unreflecting man. He was resisting, but resistance would cost him dearly in the end. What Mr. Bice had threatened might come true—he might find himself in Bodmin Gaol.

Suddenly Dorothy's voice broke in upon his reflections.

"Father," she said, trying not to betray any emotion, "what do you think?"

"Think, my child," he answered, slowly; "I think we are playing a losing game."

"Do you?" she said, with a smile. "Ah! that's because you don't know. I've come to tell you that Tom has made a discovery."

"What sort of discovery?" he asked.

"Guess, father."

"I cannot guess," he said, moodily. "I'm in no humour for guessing."

"Well, we've found that there was a secret recess in the old oaken chest. Tom made the discovery."

"Yes?" he questioned, excitedly.

"And all the deeds were there, every one of them."

"No!" with a wondering look in his eyes.

"As true as I'm here, father. What do you say now about playing a losing game?"

But he did not stay to reply. He rushed past her with an alacrity he had not shown for many a year, and was quickly by Justin's side, looking with eager and questioning eyes at the heap of papers.

For the next hour they sat around in various attitudes on the floor and on the stairs, discussing the new turn of events, and making a more minute examination of the papers.

At length Justin rose to his feet. "Look here," he said, "I'm off to Trelford."

"What for?" his father asked.

"To consult Lawyer Nankivel. There are a good many things in these papers I can't make out."

"You'll not consult Nankivel with my consent," John answered.

"Why not?" Justin asked, in surprise.

"Because he's hand and glove with old Bice. Haven't you seen it?"

Justin sat down again. "You are quite right, father," he said at length. "I can see it now that you have mentioned it."

"Exactly. Now drive over to Truro, and

bring back young Hendy with you. They tell me he's one of the smartest lawyers in the county. If the evictors turn up during your absence, we shall have an answer for them."

"They'll not turn up to-day," Justin answered from half-way down the stairs; and a quarter of an hour later he was driving rapidly away in the direction of Truro.

When Justin had disappeared, John turned to Tom and held out his hand.

"My lad," he said—and his voice shook in spite of himself—"we owe all this to you, and I'm grateful. I've not been quite fair to you in the past, I admit, but I hope you'll forgive me."

Tom took his outstretched hand and grasped it in silence.

"It was very clever of you," John went on— "very clever. I never suspected a secret drawer, and I don't think my father did before me."

"I should judge by the dates on the papers," Tom said, "that it has not been opened for nearly a hundred years."

It was late in the evening when Lawyer Hendy returned with Justin, and he had made arrangements to stay for the night. It took him several hours to go through all the documents, during which time every member of the family was on the *qui vive*.

The lawyer looked up at length and said, "The estate in dispute is larger than I thought."

"It is fully twenty acres," John replied.

"It is nearer a hundred and twenty acres," was the answer.

"That is what belonged to the Pentyres originally," John said.

"It is what belongs to the Pentyres now."

"But we've paid rent for it for the last three generations at least."

"That may be. And most likely Lord Tregeagle will endeavour to make you pay rent for it still."

"But you think the title is good?"

"It seems to me to be without a flaw. Yet I have very little doubt Lord Tregeagle will contest it. He's that sort of man."

"Then how are we to act?"

"I should advise you to take the initiative, and so bring the matter to a head at once. Tregeagle's steward, I understand, has been trying to evict you by forcible means?"

"He has."

"Then issue a summons against him for trespass, and for trying to break into your house. He will then have to show his right, and the thing will be put into train at once. I suppose you can find witnesses who saw him here?"

"Any number."

Justin clapped his hands and laughed. "Glorious!" he cried. "Evidently the fun is not all ended yet!" And so it proved; but the fun was of a very different kind.

CHAPTER XXV

THE COURSE OF LAW

" Law and equity are two things which God hath joined,
But which man hath put asunder."

In theory, as every one knows, the law is a beautiful thing. In practice an adjective of a very different kind is needed to describe it. Ostensibly laws are made in the interests of truth and justice; in reality they are made in the interests of the lawyer and the man with a long purse. There is a fable that has been long current amongst us that every man can have justice in this highly favoured land—and so he can if he is able to pay for it; but as comparatively few people are able to do that, it follows that justice is a very unfamiliar presence in many quarters, whilst the Law Courts are as much dreaded as a highway robber.

Mr. Jacob Bice knew a good deal about law. He had been trained in it from his youth. He had a certain admiration for it, as a stable-boy has for a skittish horse; its unexpected

pranks and caperings were interesting. What
it required was management. There was
nothing fixed or rigid about it. Many people
fancied so, but that was a mistake; it was as
pliant and elastic as a piece of indiarubber;
but, of course, it required a shrewd man to turn
it the right way.

In Mr. Bice's mind justice and law had little
or no connection. They were entirely separate
and distinct. Justice was a matter that he had
no concern for and took no interest in. The
beauty of law was that it enabled you to evade
justice and give it the go-by.

As a lawyer he cared nothing for mere
abstract questions of truth, and right, and equity.
Bare, obvious facts that could not be twisted
or distorted were a nuisance from his point of
view. He liked to be able to write a query
opposite every statement, then he could get
his wits to work, and perhaps set the machinery
of the law in operation. He always rejoiced
when he saw the slow movements of its wheels.
His chance came then. The lawyer was always
safe to win whatever happened. It might be
grinding widows and orphans to death, and
branding honest men as felons, and lifting rogues
and rascals into high places. That was no
concern of his. The business of the clever
lawyer was to prove—by the aid of this wonder-

T

ful machine—that wrong was right, that truth was falsehood, and that justice was a public scandal.

In the past he had rarely any cause to complain of his good fortune. Ostensibly he had worked in the interest of Lord Tregeagle, but while he had increased his employer's rent-roll, he had added very considerably to his own professional income. He had enclosed hundreds of acres of common land in the parish, and in the few cases where Lord Tregeagle's right had been disputed he had come off victor. He had evicted more than one would-be freeholder from his small estate, and had made the law such a terror to poor people generally that when he threatened them with its consequences they usually yielded up their rights without another word.

The outcome of his encounter with John Pentyre was, in his own mind, a foregone conclusion. In a few days at most he would see the farmer go under the wheels, then he would have his revenge. His surprise, therefore, was all the greater, and his indignation beyond expression, when, on the second morning after his abortive attempt at eviction, he was served with a summons for trespass and with unlawfully attempting to break into John Pentyre's house.

At first he could hardly credit his own senses. Then he raved and swore till he was nearly black in the face. Finally he condescended to make inquiries.

There was no illegality about the summons, and, rave as he might, he would have to appear before the magistrates and answer to the charge. Of course, he would be able to prove his right in five minutes; but it was terribly annoying nevertheless. It stayed the process of eviction; it made it appear to the parish as though John Pentyre had checkmated him. For the moment he would be the laughing-stock of every man and boy in the district. He wondered what Nankivel could mean by taking service for John Pentyre against him.

And he rushed off to Trelford to consult his fellow-lawyer.

Nankivel was as surprised as he. "I assure you," he said, "I have heard nothing about the matter till this moment."

"Then Pentyre has employed a fresh lawyer?"

"It seems so," he said.

"Between ourselves I don't wonder," was the cynical reply; "but I wonder what's at the bottom of it."

"Perhaps Symons knows," said Nankivel,

lugubriously; and he touched a bell for his head-clerk.

Symons came at once.

"Have you heard anything about the Pentyres, of Endilloe, since yesterday?" Nankivel questioned.

"Well, yes, sir. I heard something as I came along this morning, but I don't know if there is any truth in it."

"What did you hear?"

"Well, it is reported that young Pentyre drove over to Truro yesterday afternoon, and brought back Lawyer Hendy with him. It is also said that they have found the deeds which were missing."

"Great heavens, no!" Bice ejaculated.

"I'm only repeating what I heard as I came along, sir."

Mr. Bice did not wait to hear any more, but hurried away at once to his own office, and within half an hour he was in possession of all the facts of the case.

Later in the day he consulted his chief. Lord Tregeagle rubbed his chin for a moment, then smiled.

"In law, I think I have heard you say, Bice, it is the longest purse that wins?"

"That is so, my lord."

"Then in this matter I think we need not trouble ourselves."

"Not in the least, though, of course, as you know, law charges are always heavy."

"Yes; I am aware of that. You lawyers know how to bleed people. Still, we cannot afford to allow ourselves to be defied by a farmer; the thing is intolerable."

"We'll soon get to the end of his tether, my lord, and then his little game will be up."

"But do you think his title is of any value?"

"It may be all right in equity, sir, but what we have to do is to show that it is no good in law. That need not be difficult. You can command the best talent, and if the worst comes to the worst you can starve him out. When his lawyer finds that he has no more money he will throw up the case."

"Well, Bice, we have gone so far in this matter now that we are bound to carry it through to the end."

So the enterprise was sanctioned, the sole end and object of which was to rob an honest man of his rights, and to reduce him to a position of absolute subjection.

In the innocence of his heart, John Pentyre imagined that the matter would be settled in a week or two at the outside, and settled to his entire satisfaction. So once more he was supremely happy, and went singing to his

work as though all life's troubles had come
to an end.

Tom Pendarvis established himself at St.
Iago Churchtown as consulting engineer, and
calmly waited for clients. He was not eager
for work to come to him with a rush, for he
had brought more money with him from Africa
than he would be able to spend for many a
year; and, besides that, he was by no means
anxious that the time he spent with Dorothy
should be needlessly curtailed. Nevertheless,
as some of his inventions became known, work
crowded in upon him, and without effort on
his part he soon became a person of considerable
influence in the neighbourhood.

Justin felt almost resentful sometimes when
he saw Tom and Dorothy walking away together
across the fields in the quiet of the summer
evenings, or came upon them sitting on the
cliffs, watching the sun go down. He felt like
a bird that had lost its mate, and time, instead
of lessening the sense of his loss, seemed to
increase it.

Now that Endilloe had settled down to its
normal state of calm, and the long tension had
come to an end, he had time to brood again
over the hope that had gone out of his life.
He had loved Ruby, he believed, with a love
such as few men ever gave to a woman. His

was not an ordinary case of falling in love, it was a passion that he had resisted with might and main ; a passion that had grown upon him and dominated him in spite of himself ; a passion that neither reason nor will could defy.

An ordinary love would have expired on news reaching him of Ruby's marriage, and he would have gone his way and forgotten her, or found pleasure in the light of some other pair of eyes. But his was no ordinary love. He was quite sure of that. He could not forget her, try as he would ; and as for loving any one else, the idea seemed utterly repugnant to his nature.

St. Iago was by no means lacking in eligible maidens, some of whom would not have objected to the handsome young manager of Treskiddy Mine ; but Justin went in and out amongst them quite oblivious to their charms, and with no thought of love in his heart.

He took up his work again at the chapel with all his old interest, if not with all his old enthusiasm. He presided at tea-meetings, and entertainments, and lectures. He took part in debates and amateur Parliaments. He organized picnics and excursions, and generally lent a helping hand in all attempts at social reform.

But though he was constantly thrown into contact with the most eligible young ladies of the district, and a number of judicious mothers did their best to interest him in their daughters, he went quietly on his way, as though love and marriage were questions that never came within the circle of his thoughts.

At Dorcas meetings and such-like functions, Justin's apparent indifference to the charms of the opposite sex was a frequent subject of debate, and no one ever guessed the secret that he had so carefully hidden from prying eyes. They supposed that love had never touched him. How could they suppose any other? He had grown up amongst them; and, as far as it was known, there was not a maiden in all St. Iago that he had ever whispered a word of love to. That he should have lost his heart to Ruby Loveday never occurred to them. Very few people in the parish had even seen her. Besides, it was generally understood that she was engaged to Phil Passmore when she came, and that more recently Phil had married her. Not even Dorothy ever had a suspicion of Justin's secret. He locked it carefully in his own heart, and took no one into his confidence.

So the summer days passed away, and the year saddened into autumn, and then into winter. A new year dawned; and spring came upon the land again, and with the advent of May there was a wedding at St. Iago, and Tom and Dorothy went forth to tread the path of life together.

How happy Dorothy looked that day! She had taken her lover for better for worse, and was infinitely content. He had made a beautiful home for her not far away from Endilloe. She would be able to run home and see the old folks and Justin any time she liked. What more could she desire? Her sky was absolutely without a cloud.

Indeed, everybody appeared to be supremely happy on Dorothy's wedding-day. If now and then an anxious look came into John Pentyre's eyes, it was not on Dorothy's account. He was satisfied that Tom Pendarvis was a capital fellow, and would make Dorothy a splendid husband. No; the only thing that troubled John was that the course of English law did not run smoothly. The fate of Endilloe was still hanging in the balance, and the lawyers showed no disposition to hurry matters.

One Saturday the local paper came out with a cartoon—a most remarkable example of journalistic enterprise—in which the Endilloe estate was represented as a milch cow, with John Pentyre tugging at her horns with might and main, and Lord Tregeagle pulling at her tail with all his strength.   The lawyers meanwhile, with buckets, were milking her for dear life.

John looked at the picture and sighed.   He felt that the cartoonist had hit off the situation to a dot.

"There'll be no estate for anybody," he reflected, "if this litigation goes on much longer."

And yet not a single flaw had been found in John's title.   All the papers were in order. And in the first trial John had won.   But an appeal had been granted, and all the miserable farce had to be gone through again.

Fortunately, John had his son-in-law at his back, and Tom's purse appeared to be inexhaustible—a fact of which the lawyers appeared to be well aware, and so went cheerfully on with their arduous task, being assured that at the proper time their refreshers would not fail them.

Had the law been allowed to take its course without outside interference, it is more than probable that the longest purse would have won, and that justice would have been kicked, blindfolded, into the street—a proceeding that has become so common that it has almost ceased to excite remark.

But the case never reached the House of Lords, and for a very simple reason : Lord Treg-

eagle was summoned to appear before a Higher
Tribunal; and when his body was laid in the
family vault in St. Iago Church, his heirs and
executors refused to proceed with the case.
There was a reason for that. Lord Tregeagle
was the last of his race. With his decease the
title became extinct. But so many "next-of-kin"
appeared on the scene, and began to fight each
other with so much energy, that the case of
Endilloe was practically allowed to go by default.
The executors had enough on their hands without worrying about the rights or wrongs of John
Pentyre. The findings of the Chancery Court
were allowed to stand; and John came into possession of his own, and discovered to his joy that
the rebate of rents was almost sufficient to meet
the legal expenses; and that now, in his declining years, he was a freeholder on a somewhat
large scale, and able to hold up his head with the
best in the county.

CHAPTER XXVI

GAIN AND LOSS

"Work is not man's punishment,
It is his reward."

JUSTIN had awaited the conclusion of the trial
with intense eagerness. During the time he had
been business manager for the Bassett brothers,
he had made one or two discoveries, the most
important being that the main east and west tin
lode, which had proved such a treasure-trove to
the Bassetts, would, in the ordinary course of
things, run under a considerable portion of the
Endilloe estate; and if it was so rich in tin on
the Treskiddy side of the valley, there seemed no
reason why it should not be equally rich on the
other side.

Of course, this did not always follow. A
lode that was a perfect gold-mine in one field
might, when it passed into the adjoining field,
be absolutely worthless. Moreover, though
lodes usually ran a pretty direct course, there
were many puzzling and unfortunate exceptions.

From the fact that there were shafts in a corner of the Endilloe estate, it seemed clear that very many years before somebody had made a search for the lode on that side of the valley, and had failed to find it.

That did not prove, however, that it did not exist. A "fault" might have lifted it out of its proper course; but "faults" did not usually destroy lodes altogether. The more Justin thought about the matter, the more he felt convinced that the Treskiddy " East and West," as it was termed, ran under the Endilloe estate, and that the man who was fortunate enough to discover it would make a fortune.

Hence Justin's anxiety for the trial to end was far keener than he let any one know; and when at length his father's title was established beyond all dispute, he set to work at once to find the hidden treasure.

He made the old shaft—which he had descended years before in search of treasure of a different kind—the basis of operation. "Driving" in opposite directions, he concluded that the lode was certain to be struck sooner or later.

So the anxious days passed away, and grew into weeks, and the weeks into months, and the report from underground was always the same. No sign of the lode was visible in either direction.

Justin's father advised him to abandon the project; and more than once he was on the point of taking his father's advice, but his native tenacity of purpose came to his assistance. Having carried the search so far, it would be humiliating to give up now. It was true he had exhausted all his savings, and was borrowing from Tom Pendarvis, who was banker for the family. True also that at times hope almost failed him. And yet—and yet, for all he knew, he might be within a few inches of the coveted treasure.

"I'll try one week more," he said one day to his father, "and if that fails, then I think I'll give up, and own myself defeated."

The next day, while they were at dinner, two miners, in their working attire, came into the room unannounced.

"We've foun' un, maaster," they said, and they dived their hands into their pockets and brought out some splinters of rock.

Justin sprang to his feet in a moment, his whole frame quivering.

"Have you struck the lode?" he cried.

"Iss, maaster, we've cut 'n sure 'nough—an' a beauty tes to."

"Is this some of the ore?" he asked.

"Ay, maaster. Jest hould it up to the light an' look at it. Ain't it lovely?"

"But these are picked samples surely?"

"No, maaster. There's tons and tons of the same kind. Why, bless 'ee, maaster, the 'end' is full of it. It's the purtiest lode you've ever seen since you were born."

Justin left his dinner unfinished, and hurried away to the shaft. He wanted the testimony of his own eyes.

On the following day he took Captain Tom Bassett underground with him, who, as a practical miner, made a thorough inspection of the lode.

"Well?" Justin questioned at length.

"You needn't go to London again to make your fortune; you've got it close to your own door."

"You think it will pay for working?"

"Pay! There's nothing like it in the parish of St. Iago. I'll give you ten thousand pounds for your rights myself."

Justin drew a long breath that was almost a gasp. Ten thousand pounds! The amount seemed fabulous.

Later in the day, he went out on the cliffs and sat down. The first thrill of exultation had passed away. It was not in the power of money to satisfy the craving of the human heart. It might be some satisfaction to know that he was lifted out of the region of want—though that was a contingency that had never given him any anxiety—but beyond that there was very little to exult over.

A little way below him, on the rocks, a young miner sat with his arm round his sweetheart's waist. His whole income would not average more than fifteen shillings a week, and the girl, as a working dressmaker, would earn, perhaps, a shilling a day and her food.

Yet how happy they seemed. They listened to the deep music of the sea, untroubled about the future. They never expected riches; they had each other, and were quite content. How true it was "A man's life is not in the abundance of the things that he possesseth."

When the young couple got off the rocks and walked away along the beach towards Poldula Porth, Justin gave a long sigh. His good fortune had come too late. His first ambition to be rich was that he might win Ruby. He believed that he had no right to go to her empty-handed. He had pined for prosperity, that he might have the right to tell her of his love.

He was by no means sure now that he had not acted foolishly all the way through. He had gone upon the assumption that the main thing a girl cared for in a man was money. In reality it was the last thing she thought of if she loved him.

He had assumed also, like thousands of others, that all fortunes were a long distance away from home; and he had proved that all the while the treasure lay close to his own door.

"Well, well," he said at length, rising to his feet, "it can't be helped now. But I wonder—I wonder—what has become of her? I wonder if she is happy as Phil's wife?"

More than two years had passed away since he had heard a word respecting any of them. The Lovedays had seemed to have dropped completely out of existence, and Phil with them. No whisper of their doings ever reached Cornwall. No one appeared to know in what part of the country they had taken up their residence.

Now and then, when Justin thought of the matter, he felt surprised that Phil should content himself to live in obscurity, even though he lived in a mansion. It was not Phil's nature to hide his light under a bushel. He had always been a pushful man, with a craving for notoriety. Nothing pleased him better than seeing his name in the public press. He liked to be near the front in whatever company he might find himself. Hence this sudden and long-continued effacement was inexplicable. Could it be that he was so charmed with the company of his young wife that he desired no other; so cap-

U

tivated and fascinated by the brightness and
beauty of his own home, that he craved for no
wider world?   It might be so.   But if so, the
leopard had changed its spots and the Ethiopian
his skin.

During the next twelve months Justin had
very little time to think about any thing or any
person outside his new enterprise.   To open out
the new lode at various points, to form a company, to lay down plant, to erect "stamps," and
"buddles," and "ovens," to take the position of
manager over so many departments, absorbed
all his time, and thought, and energy.

He declared sometimes to his mother, with a
sigh of weariness, that he believed he was the
hardest-worked man in the county.

"But, my boy," she would reply, "that is
surely your own fault?"

"Not exactly, mother.   I'm bound to see the
thing through now."

"But there's such a thing as burning the
candle at both ends," she would reply.   "I
declare to father sometimes that you are getting
to look quite a middle-aged man."

"Well, I am moving on in that direction."

"Tut, tut!   You are only a youth yet."

"If a man is as old as he feels," he would
answer, with a laugh, "I declare I am not much
short of fifty."

"Then it is foolish of you to work so hard. You are a worse slave now than when you were working for your daily bread. What's the use of money if you can't get a little leisure with it?"

"Mother, that's a question I can't answer, so don't press it. But when Wheal Patience gets into working order, I shall be able to take things more quietly."

In the erection of machinery, Tom Pendarvis was given supreme command, and no one had any reason to regret the trust reposed in him. Tom entered heart and soul into the work. He was in his element, and happier than any schoolboy let loose from school.

So month by month passed away. Little by little, plant was laid down. Day by day order steadily grew out of confusion. First this machine was got to work, then that, till at length the first batch of ore was "stamped," "dressed," and sold, and then the whole district knew that Wheal Patience was a huge success.

The directors met and recommended the first dividend, and a general meeting of the shareholders was called for the following week. Justin worked early and late in preparing his report; and his mother saw, with no little anxiety, that he was exhausting his strength all too rapidly.

"What is the use, Justin," she said, "of gaining the world, and losing your life over it?"

"No use at all, mother," he answered, pathetically.

"But why do you do it?"

"I hope I am not doing it; besides, I am going in for a long rest when the general meeting is over.

He did not know how prophetic his words were. We often speak as seers without knowing it.

The general meeting was called for two o'clock. It seemed to many a red-letter day for the whole neighbourhood. Every one was in the best of spirits, and eager to hear the manager's report. Also a little proposal was on foot to present Justin with a handsome honorarium in consideration of the amount of work that he had done during the past twelve months.

While waiting for the clock to strike, the shareholders broke up into little knots and discussed Wheal Patience; discussed the price of tin, discussed Justin, discussed everything, in fact, that bore in any way upon the object of their meeting.

On the whole, Justin came in for the larger share of attention. In the eyes of many he

was regarded as something of a phenomenon.
By his persistence and energy it was believed
he had wrested Endilloe from the grasp of
Tregeagle, and certainly by the same qualities
he had discovered and developed Wheal
Patience.

Several of the older men predicted for him
a great future, and wondered where he would
live and whom he would marry, and how he
would spend his money. From a matrimonial
point of view, he was regarded as the best
catch in the neighbourhood; and the wonder
grew daily that, with all his opportunities, he
elected to remain a bachelor.

Had they known the sweet and tender
romance that he kept locked up in his heart,
they would have remained silent. But they did
not know. Justin was true to his ideal. He
had loved once, he could not love again.

The clock struck at length, and Justin had
not arrived. This was most unusual, for he
was one of the most prompt and punctual of
men. In an ante-room the directors looked at
their watches, and wondered what the manager
had done with himself.

A quarter of an hour passed away, and
still Justin had not put in an appearance.
Then one of the directors started out to make
inquiries.

He had gone underground about ten in the morning, but no one had seen him return.

Then the search was made in his private changing-room, which left no doubt that he was still underground.

By this time the anxiety had become general, and a dozen men had quickly volunteered to go underground in search of him. The meeting of the shareholders broke up in confusion; and in half an hour all St. Iago knew that Justin Pentyre was missing, and that it was feared some accident had befallen him.

CHAPTER XXVII

IN THE SHADOW

> "Life is probation, and this earth no goal,
>   But starting-point of man."

JUSTIN was found at the bottom of a newly sunk shaft, quite unconscious, and apparently dead. How he had got there was by no means clear, and he was able to volunteer no information. It was known that he was anxious to make a thorough inspection of all the "workings" before the general meeting; and it was supposed that he had missed his footing, or had been over-taken by faintness, or possibly a stave of the ladder had given way. In any case, the result had proved disastrous. He lay doubled up in a corner among the rocks. Not a moan escaped his lips, nor could the miners who found him discover the faintest symptom of life.

The news of what had happened quickly reached the surface, was carried to Endilloe, and broken gently to Justin's mother. Justin was the very light of her eyes. Yet she gave no sign of emotion, save that her lips turned suddenly pale.

"You say he is badly hurt?" she questioned, after a long pause, in a dry, hard voice.

"Yas; very badly."

"Then I must get his room ready at once. He must have the best bedroom, it is the most cheerful;" and she turned away and mounted the stairs.

The doctor was waiting at the mouth of the shaft when Justin was brought to the surface, and a brief examination showed that there was still life in him. But the extent of his injuries would have to be ascertained later.

John and Nathan and Amos came hurrying across the fields with white, haggard faces, and helped to carry Justin home.

"He's still living, mother," John said, as soon as they came into the house. "And while there's life, there's hope."

Dr. Morrison had already telegraphed to Plymouth for a trained nurse, who might be expected to arrive some time during the evening.

For the next hour a crowd of people waited downstairs and in the garden for the doctor's verdict. Conversation tapered out into absolute silence. No one was in the humour for speech.

It was all so sad and tragic. Just when

toil and effort and patient waiting had brought their reward, this had happened. The luck of the Pentyres had turned, apparently, only to turn again. And yet how little anything mattered. In the presence of death nothing was of any value. Men gained the world, and lost their lives. They heaped up treasures for others to gather.

Dorothy came downstairs at length, with red eyes and trembling lips.

"He is living," she said brokenly, in reply to a dozen inquiries; "and that is about all that can be said. Dr. Morrison says he is terribly hurt. His right leg is broken, and his left shoulder dislocated. But that is not the worst. His head is severely injured, and the doctor is unable to say at present whether it is a case of fractured skull, or merely concussion of the brain."

"And is he still unconscious?" some one questioned.

"Quite ; but he is not in a state of coma. He talks constantly; yet he has not the remotest idea where he is, or what has happened to him."

So the little crowd dispersed sadly and silently to their homes and to their work, and Dr. Morrison kept anxious watch by Justin's bedside.

It was late in the evening, and quite dark

when the nurse arrived; a dainty, girlish figure, who ran lightly upstairs and into the sick-room as though she knew the way well.

Dr. Morrison met her with a very grave face, and gave her careful and minute instructions which she would have to carry out during the night.

"You have had experience in accident cases?" he questioned.

"Yes; a good deal."

"You look very young."

"I have had three years of hospital work," was the reply.

"Ah, that will do. I need not tell you that a good deal will depend upon nursing in this case."

"Is it a very bad case?"

"I fear so. But it is impossible to determine just yet the extent of the injuries."

"If careful nursing can pull him through," she said, with a little choke in her voice, "then he will get better."

When the doctor had left, she raised the shade of the lamp a little, so that the light fell on the sufferer's face. Then she went close to the bedside and bent over him.

Justin lay quite still, with closed eyes, but his breathing was heavy and laboured, and his brow was contracted as if he were in pain.

The nurse looked at him for a long time without moving, save that once or twice she raised her hand to her eyes as if to wipe away a sudden tear. The sight of this strong, handsome fellow hovering upon the brink of death had evidently touched her sensitive nature. She gave a sigh at length and turned away from the bed and shifted the lamp-shade so that the light no longer fell on Justin's face.

Half an hour later Justin's father and mother came into the room, and sat for a long time, one on each side of the bed, looking wistfully at the face of their boy, but speaking no word. The nurse, with her face in shadow, watched them intently, but they took very little notice of her.

They stole away at length on tip-toe after a whispered good night; and for a long time the house was wrapped in a great silence.

The nurse drew up her chair near the bed, and watched with curious and sympathetic eagerness every expression that passed over the face of her patient.

Soon after midnight Justin opened his eyes and began to talk. At first he appeared to be addressing a meeting of shareholders, then he began to argue with some one who wanted to steal the farm, and got quite excited over the matter.

The nurse rose at once, and laid her hand on his forehead.

Instantly he turned his eyes, and looked her straight in the face.

"Who are you?" he began; then he paused, and for awhile was silent. "No, no," he went on at length, "you are not old enough or strong enough for our work. Besides, we have taken on all the hands we can employ on the floors at present—'Count House maid, eh?" and he laughed softly. "Well, no. I should have all the neighbourhood talking in a week."

Then he closed his eyes and began to soliloquize. "Pretty girl, that—very pretty girl— reminds me something of Ruby—Ruby—Ruby;" and he repeated the name over and over again softly to himself.

"They wonder I didn't get married," he said at length, with a smile. "But I never shall. If I had never seen Ruby, things might have been different. Ah! Ruby—Ruby—" and his voice ended in a whisper.

The nurse turned and walked to the other end of the room. Such confidences were not for her, and yet she could not help hearing.

Justin grew quiet at length, and lay quite still, as if asleep. The nurse came back and stood close to his bedside again, and for the best part of an hour she never once lifted her eyes from his face.

The doctor was back again with the dawn, and the household was stirring early. The nurse was ordered to bed as soon as Mrs. Pentyre could take her place. Dorothy came across from her own house as soon as she could get away.

Dorothy and the nurse came face to face on the top of the stairs. The recognition was instantaneous and complete.

"Ruby!" Dorothy cried in astonishment.

"Yes, Dorothy;" and the next moment they fell to kissing each other and crying, as though these were the only ways open to them of expressing their emotion.

Ruby was the first to recover herself. "Come into my room, Dorothy," she said, "and let us talk; I can't sleep yet if I go to bed."

Dorothy followed without a word. She was too astonished yet even to ask questions.

"You are surprised to see me here," Ruby said, as soon as they were seated opposite one another.

"Very much. I do not understand it at all. Why are you a nurse?"

"I had to do something for a living," was the reply, "and nursing was the only thing I had a talent for."

"But—but—what of your husband? Does he approve?"

"My husband did you say?—my husband——?"

"Yes; you are married, are you not?" And Dorothy glanced curiously at Ruby's hands, which were perfectly innocent of rings.

"Ruby gave a little laugh. "No, Dorothy," she said, "I am not married; whatever could have put such an idea into your head?"

"But it was stated in the papers that you were married."

"Stated in the papers?" she questioned, with increasing surprise.

"Why, yes. It must be three years ago now or more. It was said that you and Phil were married, and had gone on the Continent for your honeymoon."

Ruby rose to her feet, her face very white and her hands trembling.

"Did you believe that I had married Phil Passmore?" she questioned, eagerly.

"Why, of course we did, Ruby. What else could we believe?"

"And did he—that is, did—did—your brother believe it?"

"I suppose so. Why shouldn't he? We none of us had any reason for doubting it. But we did wonder that you never sent us a line."

Ruby sat down again, and breathed hard. "Phil Passmore is your cousin," she said at length. "And after—after what had happened, I felt I could not write."

"Why?" Dorothy asked, simply.

"Why! Do you not know that he ruined my father? That—that—— Oh, I cannot tell you everything."

It was now Dorothy's turn to look surprised.

"I do not understand you," she said. "What has Phil done? We have not heard a whisper about him for years."

Ruby clasped and unclasped her hands nervously, and her lips trembled, in spite of all her efforts to control herself.

"Father trusted him implicitly," she said, after a long pause; "and then came the crash, and father had to pay everything. I do not understand it. Your cousin got quite clear somehow—not even did his name appear. He professed that he was only a clerk in the firm of Mead, Runcorn, and Jago, and somehow those individuals could not be found. Oh, it was an awful time of it. We had to give up our house in Regent's Park, and go into a little house in Brondesbury. And then father fell ill, and in three weeks he was dead——"

"Oh, I did not know," Dorothy said, sympathetically. "I am very sorry."

"Your cousin never came near us," Ruby went on at length; "but we heard that he blossomed out in greater style than ever, and set up an expensive establishment in the West End. It did not take long to settle up poor father's affairs, and then mother and I found ourselves almost penniless. Mother has a little money of her own that grandfather left her, so she decided to go and live with Aunt Jane. But I have nothing; that is the reason I became a nurse."

Dorothy drew her chair close up to her friend and kissed her.

"Oh, Ruby, I am grieved for you," she said. "We had all thought things were so very different. I do not wonder that you did not write to us. But please don't think evil of us because Phil is our relative."

"I do not, Dorothy. Please do not imagine that. No, no; it was not that. But when one is down, it is not easy to write. You cannot explain things very well, and so you keep silence."

"We have often talked about you," Dorothy said at length, "and wondered how you were."

"Then you had not quite forgotten me?" Ruby questioned, with a pathetic smile.

"Forgotten you! Oh no, Ruby, we were not likely to do that. But you must get some sleep now, for you will need all your strength if you are to pull Justin round. How strange, that of all the nurses in the country the lot should have fallen on you."

"Well, you see, I was the only one in the hospital available when the telegram came."

"And you knew you were coming here?"

"Not till three minutes before I started. I was told to get ready to go into Cornwall by the next train. The address was given to me when I was ready to start."

"It seems a curious chance, or Providence, or whatever you like to call it," Dorothy said, reflectively.

"Perhaps in return for saving my life," Ruby answered, "I may be permitted to help in saving his."

"Oh, I hope you will, Ruby. Justin deserves to live. He has worked so hard, and striven so heroically, that it would seem such a mistake and such a waste if he were to die."

Ruby thought so too, but she made no reply, and soon after Dorothy left her. She shut her eyes and tried her best to court sleep, but sleep would not come. Her brain and heart were in a tumult. It seemed so strange that, after all these years, she should come back to nurse the man who had saved her life—the man whose image had been impressed on her brain ever since; the one man she had ever cared for.

She wondered again if he had cared for her.

x

During the few times he had called upon them in London she had sometimes fancied that the look in his eyes meant more than mere friendship. But in his speech he had been very reticent, and his manner was almost shy.

Now again, in his delirium, he had mentioned her name, and mentioned it in such a way as to make her heart throb wildly. Yet she knew that in such cases people often said the very opposite of what they meant. Hence it was foolish to speculate on the ravings of a man who was suffering from concussion of the brain.

When, two hours later, she went back into Justin's room, she found him apparently in a state of coma. The doctor sat by his side with his fingers on his wrist.

"He keeps up his strength fairly well," he said, without looking up. "But it will need all our patience and skill, nurse, to pull him through."

"Then perhaps we shall succeed, doctor," she said, with a smile. "You will supply the skill and I will supply the patience."

He turned and looked at her with a start. Something in the tones of her voice struck him as being familiar.

"Have we met before?" he asked abruptly.

"Then you have forgotten me?" she said, looking up at him and smiling.

"By Jove! Yes, and no. When have we met before?"

"In this house and in this very room. Don't you remember doctoring my sprained ankle?"

"What! are you Ruby Loveday?"

"The same."

"Of course you are. Good gracious! But— but——"

"Dorothy will tell you all about it," she said, with a smile.

"I think we shall succeed now," he said, with a grunt, and he hurried out of the room.

CHAPTER XXVIII

DARKNESS AND DAWN

"Love lieth deep   .   .   .
    Love laps his wings on either side the heart."

JUSTIN remained in the darkness of mental night
for fifteen days.   Then after a sleep so long
and so profound that the doctor feared he
would never wake again, he opened his eyes
and looked curiously round him.   It was late
afternoon, and the room was full of a soft,
subdued light.   Not a sound broke the stillness
except the ticking of a small clock on the
mantelpiece.   Ruby sat some distance away,
with her face bent over a book.

Justin glanced from side to side for several
seconds, unable to make out where he was,
then he recognized the furniture of the best
bedroom, but that scarcely helped him.   Why
was he in that room at all, and why was he
in bed?

He tried to raise himself on his elbow at
length, but fell back with a low moan.   Instantly

Ruby dropped her book and came to his side. Her back was towards the window, so that he could scarcely see her face. She saw, however, that he was conscious, and a strange thrill of joy ran through her.

"Why am I here, and who are you?" he asked, abruptly.

"You have been ill," she said, in a whisper, "and I am your nurse. Now, take this and you will feel better."

He opened his mouth and swallowed the medicine without the faintest protest, but he did not take his eyes from her face for a moment.

"Have I been very ill?" he questioned. "I feel curiously weak."

"You met with an accident," she said, in the same low whisper, "but you are getting on nicely."

"Ah, yes, I remember. That was this morning. I wonder how I am to get to the meeting?"

"The meeting has been postponed," she answered, "until you are quite well. Now you must keep perfectly still and not worry yourself."

He closed his eyes and kept them shut for several minutes. But she saw by his knitted brows that his brain was active.

"Would you mind telling me," he said at length, "what day it is?"

"It is Wednesday," she answered, still keeping her voice to a whisper, for she did not want him to recognize her just yet.

"Wednesday?" he answered, feebly. "Then I've been off my head since yesterday."

"You had a bad fall, and were quite unconscious when found."

"Oh, I see," he said, reflectively. "And what's the matter with my leg?"

"Broken," she answered, straightening the counterpane.

"And my shoulder—is that broken also?"

"Oh no, that was only dislocated. I dare say it feels a little stiff and sore, but it will soon be all right again."

"And are there any other breakages?" he asked, with a pathetic smile.

"No, I don't think so. You have only to be patient and obey orders, and you'll soon be all right again."

"But where is my mother?" he asked.

"She is resting now. She has been with you all the morning, but you were fast asleep."

"And have you only just come?"

"Dr. Morrison telegraphed to Plymouth as soon as it was known you had met with an accident, and I was sent off at once."

"Then you are a regular hospital nurse?"

"Yes."

"Been in the work long?"

"Three years." And she turned away, and went to the window and drew up the blind and let a little more light into the room.

Justin watched her with a wondering expression in his eyes. He was too weak to think very clearly or consecutively, and yet in a hundred ways this low-voiced nurse reminded him of Ruby.

He closed his eyes at length, and tried to live over again some of the old days, when hope burnt like a star on the horizon of his life.

Ruby came back to his bed again after a few minutes, with a glass of jelly and a spoon.

"Now you must take this," she said, with a curious little shake in her voice. "If you are to get well quickly, you must take all the nourishment you can."

He opened his eyes, and looked at her without speaking. She reminded him of Ruby more than ever. They might be twin sisters.

"You are very much like a friend of ours," he said, after he had taken two or three spoonfuls of jelly.

"Indeed."

"I should swear you are the same," he said, "only, of course, I know you cannot be."

Her hand trembled as she passed the spoon again to his lips, but she did not speak.

"I never saw two people so much alike," he went on. "It is quite perplexing."

"What was your friend's name?" she asked.

"Ruby," he said, faintly. "Ruby Loveday."

"My name is Ruby," she answered, in a whisper.

He turned his head slightly—he had no strength to do more—and looked at her again. Then their eyes met in a revealing glance.

"Ah!" he said, with a little gasp. "Then I am not mistaken. You are Ruby, but not Ruby Loveday."

"Yes, I am Ruby Loveday," she answered, with a pathetic smile. "No; please do not talk any more now. I am afraid you have already talked too much. When you are stronger you shall know all you want to know."

"No, no," he whispered, pleadingly. "Tell me now. I shall worry if you don't."

"Then close your eyes and keep very still. There is not very much to be told. Father trusted your cousin, Mr. Passmore, and lost everything. I think it broke his heart. He died three years ago. So mother went to live with her sister, and I have earned my living ever since as a nurse. How the report got about that I was married, I do not know. It is utterly false. I would sooner have died any time than married Phil Passmore. Now you know everything. Don't ask any more questions now, but get some sleep if you can."

He opened his eyes and smiled at her, then with a whispered "thank you," closed them again, and soon after he seemed to be fast asleep.

*   *   *   *   *

A week later, not only Ruby, but the doctor had nearly given up hope. Justin had recovered consciousness and gladdened the hearts of his father and mother and Dorothy by recognizing them again, but he did not recover strength. Day by day he grew weaker, and it seemed as if nothing on earth could save him. He lay quite still without a moan and without ever a word of regret. Now and then he smiled at his mother and the rest, but he was too weak to talk, or the effort seemed too great for him to make.

It was nearly an hour past midnight, and Ruby was watching by his side. She was nearly heart-broken. She had hoped that she might repay him for saving her life by helping to save his, but it seemed as if it were not to be. If ever nursing was a labour of love,

it was so in her case. She had cherished
his memory for years. All the romance of
her life had gathered round his name. From
the day he had plucked her out of the hands
of the cruel sea, and had carried her home
through the moonlight in his strong arms, and
she had felt his cheek close to hers—there
had been no other in the world that could
compare with him. His very reticence and
apparent coldness seemed but to increase her
love for him. He was so different from the
shallow, flippant youths who gathered round
her and paid her silly compliments. He was
strong and reliant, and a man to be trusted.
He feared God and reverenced his parents, and
was as devoted as a lover to his sister. Such
a man was worth knowing and worth loving.

And yet she did not dream of love at first.
She admired him and reverenced him. But out
of reverence, love grew little by little. She
found herself dreaming about him and hoping
she would meet him. And when disaster over-
took her father, she almost pined for a sight of
his face, for she felt sure they would have his
sympathy.

Then followed silent years of toil; and when
she came as far west as Plymouth, she wondered
if they would ever meet again. Justin was her
ideal still—the one man she could ever love.

Was it Providence that she should have been sent to nurse him? She almost thought so at first. God was good to her, and was going to allow her to pay a debt that long had lain upon her heart.

But now, as she sat watching him in the solemn hush of the night, it almost seemed as though Providence were mocking her. They had met but to part again for ever.

"Ruby!" The word fell faint upon her ear as the sighing of a zephyr. "Will you come a little nearer? I want to talk to you."

She gulped down a sob that had risen in her throat, and was by his side in a moment.

"I think I shall not get better," he went on, faintly. "I seem to be slipping out of life."

"No, no, don't say that," she answered, chokingly. "You must not give up hope."

"I have tried not, but—but—well, it cannot be helped," he whispered faintly; "but I want to tell you something before I go."

She bent over him with eyes brimful of tears, but did not answer him.

"Perhaps I ought to be thinking of other things," he went on, "but I cannot help telling you, Ruby. I have loved you ever since that night I found you on the beach. Loved you! Ah! none but God can tell how much I have loved you. I went to London that I might be near you, and in spite of circumstances I clung to the hope that I might win you. What I suffered during that fruitless struggle no one will ever know. Then I missed you and found your house empty, and it was rumoured that you were married. So I turned my back upon London, which I had endured only because of my love for you. It was sweet to come home again, and for years I have worked, glad that I had loved even though I had lost.

"It was strange that you should find me here. I think it was God who sent you. And for weeks you have nursed me with patient kindness. And I have not minded the suffering since you were near me. I hope you do not think I do wrong in telling you this, Ruby. No harm can come of your knowing that I have loved you and that I love you still.

"I know I was never worthy of you, Ruby, but that does not matter now——"

Suddenly she lifted her face, while the tears streamed down her cheeks.

"Hush! hush!" she cried. "You must never say that again or even think it. Not worthy of me! Oh, Justin——" and she dropped on her knees and buried her face in the bed-clothes.

For awhile the silence was broken only by Ruby's sobs.

Then Justin spoke again in the faintest whisper.

"Don't cry," he said; "I did not mean to pain you."

"I won't cry if you will get better," she said, smiling at him through her tears. "If you love me you must get well again for my sake."

He reached out his wasted hand to her, and she took it in both of hers and kissed it.

Then he understood, and soon after he fell asleep again.

For another twenty-four hours his life trembled in the balance. Ruby, Dorothy, and his mother watched by him with infinite solicitude and with unfailing patience and love; and when at length the tide of life that had ebbed out so far began to flow back again, old Dr. Morrison rubbed his hands and declared that it was the nursing that had done it.

Summer was quite over when Justin was able to get downstairs again. But Nature is generous in that western county, and there were lovely autumnal days when the sun shone out of a cloudless sky and not a leaf stirred on the trees, when the flowers still bloomed in the garden, and the air was like nectar.

Ruby would remind Justin of the days when she was the invalid and he was her good and gallant knight, and he would look at her and smile, for speech was too clumsy a medium to reveal what was in his heart.

Those were happy days for both. Before the days of fog and rain came on, he was able to get as far as the cliffs, and listen again to the deep music of the sea. All restraint had long since disappeared, and they talked as lovers should.

Ruby did not go back again to Plymouth, but she went on a long visit to Dorothy, and helped her to nurse her firstborn. During the spring a new wing was added to Endilloe, and then the people of St. Iago began to talk, and to put two and two together, and to prophesy.

Nathan was still convinced of the general ignorance of townspeople, but he admitted that Ruby was an exception.

"She's what I call a beauty," he said to Amos. "A purtier, or a sweeter, or a brighter little maid I've never seed; an' if I'd been forty year younger I should ha' tumbled in love with her myself."

Early in March Amos got his heart's desire and more. His son Dan'l came home for a visit, bringing his bride with him—a happy, good-looking, light-hearted lass, who turned all her a's into i's, and all her r's into w's, and who went into raptures over everything she saw.

Amos laughed till the tears ran down his face,

and when Dan'l's wife kissed him, he blushed till his face was scarlet.

Nathan received quite a shock when he saw Dan'l. The freckled, loutish youth had become a smart, well-dressed man, who evidently had all his wits about him.

"I'm not goin' to say, Amos," he said, "that your Dan'l ain't terribly improved; but then you know he growed up in the country, and that makes oal the difference."

"But look at his wife," said Amos, in triumph. "An' she was born up there in that big town."

But Nathan vouchsafed no answer; the problem was beyond him.

Had a stranger been passing through St. Iago one morning early in May he would have discovered that something unusual had happened, or was happening. The whole place had quite a festive appearance. Bunting was flying from the engine-houses, and from the top of the "shears," and from stump frames, and from the counting-house windows. The village street was thronged with boys and girls. The Methodist chapel was crowded to its utmost capacity, while so many carriages with grey horses attached had never been seen in St. Iago before.

Justin was still pale, and walked with just

a perceptible limp when he left the chapel with his happy young bride leaning on his arm. Ruby looked younger and lovelier than ever.

Over the breakfast-table there was a good deal of speech-making, and when Justin, in reply to the toast "The health of the bride and bridegroom," said, "I went away to seek my fortune, and came home to find it," there was a burst of cheering that could be heard to the end of the garden. Some thought of the fortune in Wheal Patience Mine, and some thought of Ruby. But those who were watching Justin closely, and saw the look in his eyes as he glanced towards his beautiful young wife, knew well enough what was in his heart.

He did not despise the rich acres of Endilloe, nor the wealth in Wheal Patience Mine, but Ruby was more to him than everything else on earth.

THE END

PRINTED BY WILLIAM CLOWES AND SONS, LIMITED,
LONDON AND BECCLES.

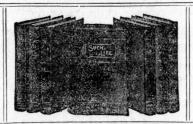

Silas K. Hocking's Popular Works.

In large crown 8vo, cloth gilt, bevelled boards, price 3s. 6d. each. (In uniform style.)

THE HEART OF MAN. With Original Illustrations by ERNEST PRATER.

The Free Methodist says: "Should Mr. Hocking write no more, his niche in English literature is now filled. Taken in every way, the book is great. Arrestive, sustained, idyllic, powerfully dramatic, it lays hold of the reader from the first and holds him as with a spell. 'The Heart of Man' is true to its title. We are face to face with the issues of life, but we are face to face with them in the home, in the street, in the church, and not in the schools."

A SON OF REUBEN. With Original Illustrations by H. R. STEER, R.I.

The Aberdeen Free Press says: "It may be confidently predicted that this charming story will be reckoned as one of the best of this popular writer's works. It is not surprising to learn, as was noted the other day, the immense circulation his books have attained, and it is no exaggerated praise to say that 'A Son of Reuben' will take its place among the best of them."

ONE IN CHARITY. With Original Illustrations by GORDON BROWNE.

The Western Morning News says: "A capital story of unusual interest. There is an air of naturalness and freedom in the whole story, which will make it pleasant reading for old and young alike."

CALEB CARTHEW: A Life Story. With Original Illustrations by LANCELOT SPEED.

The Morning Post says: "'Caleb Carthew' is no ordinary book, and the best may yet learn much that is good from its perusal. An earnest manly tone runs through it."

FOR ABIGAIL: A West-Country Story. With Original Illustrations by W. S. STACEY.

The Academy says: "'For Abigail' reminds us, to an extent, of 'John Halifax,' and its author will not care for higher commendation."

WHERE DUTY LIES. With Original Illustrations by HAROLD COPPING.

The Glasgow Herald says: "The story is one of great and sustained interest, with plenty of movement and mystery. The illustrations, from original drawings by Harold Copping, form a pleasing feature."

FOR LIGHT AND LIBERTY. With Original Illustrations by ALFRED JOHNSON.

The Publishers' Circular says: "With a keen remembrance of Mr. Hocking's other works of fiction, we are inclined to think he has never imagined or written anything better than this."

A Special Illustrated Edition, in medium 8vo, cloth gilt, 3s. 6d.

HER BENNY: A Story of Street Life. Illustrated with 47 Original Engravings.

The Spectator says: "This is a beautifully got-up edition of a most pathetic tale. There are few, if any, tales better than this one."

This story is also issued at 2s. 6d., uniform style with the undermentioned volumes.

In crown 8vo, cloth gilt, gilt edges, uniform style, price 2s. 6d.

IVY: A Tale of Cottage Life. With Six Original Illustrations.

The Edinburgh Courant says: "This is a homely story, told in simple language. The book deserves praise for its form; the printing is good, the illustrations beautiful, and the binding very tasteful."

Silas K. Hocking's Popular Works.

In crown 8vo, cloth gilt, gilt edges, uniform style, price 2s. 6d. each.

HIS FATHER; or, A Mother's Legacy. With numerous Original Illustrations.

The Record says: "A pathetic and interesting tale."

ALEC GREEN: A Story of Cornish Life. With Six Original Illustrations.

The Hampshire Advertiser says: "A good readable book. . . . The author has conveyed the lesson he wished to teach in an interesting manner."

SEA WAIF: A Tale of the Sea. With Six Original Illustrations.

The Plymouth W.D.M. says: "The narrative abounds in interesting incidents, and is written with a vigorous and graphic pen throughout."

DICK'S FAIRY: A Tale of the Streets. With Six Original Illustrations.

The St. James's Gazette says: "The moral of the book is excellent."

CRICKET: A Tale of Humble Life. With Six Original Illustrations.

The Times says: "It is an excellent story, capitally told."

TREGEAGLE'S HEAD: A Tale of the Cornish Coast With Six Original Illustrations.

The Southport Visitor says: "There is much variety and fascination in the story. The plot is a remarkably ingenious one."

CROOKLEIGH: A Village Story. With Six Original Illustrations by W. S. STACEY.

The Huddersfield Examiner says: "It is one of the most straightforward, simple-hearted, common-sense tales that we have seen."

REAL GRIT. With Six Original Illustrations by F. BARNARD.

The Birmingham Daily Gazette says: "The fame of this author is almost too well known to need even a word from the reviewer, but 'Real Grit' is too beautiful to pass over. Those who have read it will recommend it; those who have not will be wise to get it."

REEDYFORD; or, Creed and Character. With Six Original Illustrations.

The Scotsman says: "The story is vigorously and pathetically told, and will enhance the author's reputation."

"CHIPS," JOE, AND MIKE. With numerous Original Illustrations.

The Nonconformist says: "Will touch the hearts of all who may read it."
The Sentinel says: "Most suitable for adding to school and village libraries."

REX REYNOR, ARTIST: A Story of Sowing and Reaping. With Six Original Illustrations by HAROLD COPPING.

The Birmingham Daily Gazette says: "The story is well told; the characters are natural. It is a volume which can be read and re-read with unflagging interest."